Silver Haven

Silver Haven

R.A. Robinson

Copyright© 2004 Rachel Baldwin

LOC
ISBN 0-89716-816-x

First printing
10 9 8 7 6 5 4 3 2 1

Layout by Ordgruppen, Stockholm, Sweden
Printed at Författares Bokmaskin, Stockholm, Sweden

THIS BOOK IS DEDICATED

To the memory of all my family and friends I have touched in my life, that longer walk among us.

To my husband for all his love, understanding and continued support to follow my dream, and to bring my stories to life.

ACKNOWLEDGMENTS

To my dear family, for there continued
support and love.

To my loving husband. For his understanding, and patience.

To all my friends for the parts they played
in my life, to write my stories.

I thank you, one and all for being
part of my world.

INTRODUCTION

This is a story about the after math of a major disaster of our planet. It's about families that survived and what they had to deal with on a world where nothing was left living on the surface.

We will explore the lives of our brave family and watch them work through trails and tribulations to continue to survive on a dead world.

We will meet other groups of survivors and have to decide how to handle each situation carefully.

Our family will grow with births, and bringing in other people we find upon our patrols of the new uncharted territory.

Come with us on the journey to rebuild earth, and make it a better place than before.

CHAPTER 1

We knew of a giant comet speeding toward earth for some time, however, like most of us, we thought and hoped it would miss us like so many others in the past. But we were wrong.

It took over a year for the dust to settle, after the great comet hit our planet earth in the year 2199. It struck full impact over Russia and the upper Siberian region.

Some had time to prepare for it; we knew it was going to hit us for many months. We had college students in our group so they were telling us for a long time to start stockpiling supplies, for it would be a long stay under ground. The main thing was to find the perfect place for a group to stay for perhaps years.

The major governments combined efforts tried everything known to man, to stop it, but to know avail. It was no use, the comet kept coming and soon it was clear to everyone that it was going to hit, hard and fast. We busied ourselves with planning and gathering all the necessary information for a long underground haul.

All people, animals and plant life left on the planet surface were killed quickly. The shock wave covered the entire planet and within a matter of weeks, there was no vegetation left. Everything died off within a very short period of time, due to lack of food, good drinking water and sunlight. There was a blanket of thick orange dust covering everything, plus low levels of radiation and then the acid rain.

There are pockets of large families, communities, and other people that went under ground all over the planet. But with all communications destroyed and survival being the number one priority, everyone stayed close to their groups.

We all know that the current governments around the world at that time would have gone underground and lived, perhaps even thrived. The very wealthy and the very smart would live through it, but for how long and in what type of conditions as time goes on, who knows for sure.

I guess we would be the smart ones. We had some very smart people in our group. Some were mere friends of the families. They decided to stay with us. Others just got caught up in the whole idea of the end of the world, as we know it and were scared to leave.

Some of the braver souls ventured out only to return, shaking their heads, "there is nothing left, everything is gone." And sometimes, not coming back to us at all.

We are a group of an extended family of 28, men,

women and children. We scouted out the hills around our homes for some time and planned for the day of darkness we called it. We took turns digging into the hills of Montana, an old abandon silver mine.

We call our home, "Silver Haven."

It was a lot of work from all of us to set things up at first and try to keep things as low key as possible, we did not want to arouse a lot of interest in our project, for we were planning it around a small number of people. We made sure we had more than enough in the way of supplies and materials for the long underground stay.

We truly didn't know how long we could be staying in this place.

What might the conditions of the earth be in after things started to come back to life, if it did at all? So many questions that we had no real answers for, we just had to take one day at a time and try to make the best of it. Only time would tell, how earth would come back and start anew. We prayed for hope, and renewed life.

For the first few months under ground there was plenty to keep us all busy. We set up our sleeping areas, kitchen, latrine and even a bath. We explored the mine completely and found some interesting things. We dug new tunnels and opened up old mine shafts. We made sure that all the shafts were re-enforced and stabilized. We even had time for some mining of the silver that was still in the mine. In the long winters it gave the men something to do and kept them fit. You never know if silver would be worth something in

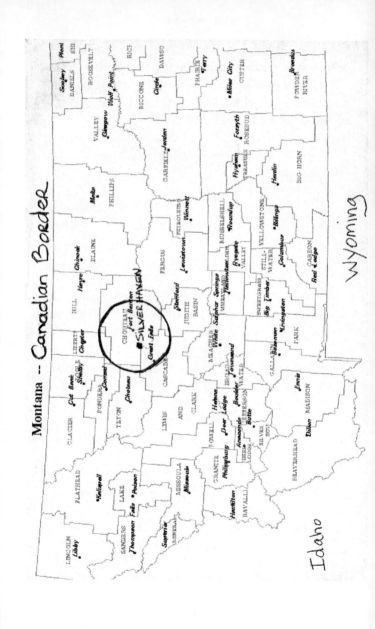

the new world. The walls in some of the tunnels still had traces of silver. We ran a rope handrail throughout the entire tunnel network. It took weeks and miles of rope.

We found an under ground stream of good, fresh drinking water, deep in one of the lower junctions, which flowed down into a clear pool. We all thanked god for this blessing and prayed more to come as the months passed. We ran miles of pipe and tubes from the stream to the garden and animals. Plus we attached a tube to a large plastic drum for drinking and cooking water. We had rolled down over a dozen hundred-gallon drums of fuel that ran the two generators. We only used these for cooking and our heat lamps. We have thousands of candles, which light our halls and tunnels, which are monitored daily, by the children in a game.

A back wall was built with shelves on it, to store our batteries, for other lighting, cooking and emergencies, which we use sparingly. They had to be recharged off one another regularly. All these daily functions were run and handled by our group.

We created a quiet room with lots of board games, and wall-to-wall shelves full of books of every possible topic. There were large comfortable chairs and different size tables. There is a large chest full of every map of the world and detailed maps of the United States and many of our state of Montana and surrounding states.

We would spend our free time here, reading was the favorite of most of the adults, and there were paints and two isles for anyone interested in creating art for our home. We had reams of paper for journals, writing, notes and just putting down individual thoughts. We had buckets of colored pens and boxes of sharpened pencils and color crayons.

My mother Esther, father Leo, brother Joseph, sister Leah and myself Rachel, shared one large alcove near the far corner surrounding the pool. We each had our cots with sleeping bags and small bookcase or boxes for our personal belongings. We hung bright curtains to give us all a little privacy. We had candles in little cut outs in the rock walls and I had a mirror in another one.

One of the big projects was working on starting up the garden. With the help of the grow lights and water from the pool, we irrigated. The soil is rich and sand we carried down in buckets from outside that made for great, fruits and vegetables all year round. We also used the animals dung for fertilizer. Fresh mushrooms grew wild everywhere and all this helped with our fresh air system.

We arranged charcoal filters in a system that was vented out lots of small holds in the mountainside. The entrance was guarded around the clock with an armed man. A large boulder sealed everything inside, which we put on a rail to roll it back and forth from the inside only. We all felt very secure and safe in our mountainside home.

Another family took care of preparing our meals, six in their family. Another family took care of our livestock and weapons; there are seven of them in all.

We have nine single men of all ages, and one woman who we call sister Sarah our minister and doctor. She made sure that we had plenty of medical supplies. It was easy for her to get some of the drugs for she was a nurse in a major hospital.

The men all take turns at the entrance and we all work together to keep our group alive and well during this challenging time of our lives and planet.

We try to do things together as groups and we become very close knit and I think we work well together as a team or large family. We really only have each other with lots of time, to think, to work and to make our surroundings a better place to live in.

We have been closed in for some time now and some of us are starting to go stir crazy. The guys explore the tunnels more and more, finding all sorts of abandon tools, lanterns and mining equipment. We use everything, and nothing is wasted. They were mining silver more each day too, but after a while, even that was not enough to keep their minds from wandering topside.

One day on their excavations of a new tunnel we hear yelling for help down the tunnel. "Rachel come quick, I need your help." Sarah shouts leaning over Damien. He is rolling on the ground holding his leg. "What is it?" I ask as I come running toward them. "Damien has been bitten by a snake, hold him down while I lance it to release the poison." Sarah says taking a small sharp knife from her medical kit. I take his head and holding his hands, I watch Sarah work quickly, bending over his leg and then pours disinfected on the puncture wound. She spits out the poison.

Damien begins to sweat and toss his head back and forth with fever. Jason and Aaron rush in carrying a cot, lifting him on to it, they carry him back to his sleeping area, while Sarah mixes up something for him to drink. We all stay close for hours waiting for a change, or the fever to break.

John the oldest of the single men's group, comes back from his rounds to see the commotion. "What's happened here," he asks Sarah now wiping Damien's damp face. She stands and takes him by the arm, walking away talking in whispers.

Daniel leaves the group to go on watch, "take care of my brother until I get back." Everyone nods to him in unison and turn back to look after Damien. We all take turns watching him through the night. It is a very restless night for everyone.

The following morning John organizes a snake hunt and everyone is invited to join in the day's task of ridding the tunnels and encampment of the poisonous snakes once and for all. We wrapped our legs in leather and carried bags and very long sharp knives. We turn over every rock we can find and go down every tunnel. We climb up into the ledges and feel around in the holes.

By afternoon I go back to check on Damien and I notice that his fever has broken, so I sit down by him for a while. I fix his pillow, wipe his face and watch over him.

Shortly Sarah shows up with another cup of medicine. Damien wakes up and swallows down the liquid. He starts to make a slow recovery, with the help of everyone. Our quick response to this accident, helped save his life. With our teamwork and professionalism, we all work together and this is what makes us strong and we will survive.

By evening Susan goes running into the kitchen to help her mother Janice, and father David fix dinner. Everyone returns from the hunt with bags of snakes. "There was a den of them, I am glad we got them now, or we would have been over run with them soon." John says to everyone at dinner. "I hope we bagged them all. Maybe they will find a way topside and die for lack of food. Only time will tell. I think they have been eating the rats too. Which was not a bad thing. So now I hope we are not over run with rats." We settle down to eat dinner and discuss what to do with the snakes.

"I hear snake is good eating and it tastes just like chicken." David chuckles. "Besides it's another source of fresh meat for us. I think I can prepare them properly with the help of the boys doing the beheading and skinning. I will do the rest." David smiles and waits for a decision.

"Okay, David, if you think it's safe and you can make meals of them." John says and nods to the boys to take them to the kitchen and help him with the work after dinner.

We all eat two meals a day. Morning and evening, but the three little children are given an afternoon snack. Brother and sister Dale and Donna are a year apart, he is ten she is nine, and the baby of the group is little Denise she is six. Their mother Jane and father Sam tend to the livestock and maintain the weapons locker with John as over seeing them with routine inventory and cleaning.

The following nights dinner was really delicious, we all ate snake for the first time it was a very tasty meal. David and Janice were very proud of their culinary success. Everyone was delighted with the change in diet and the fact they ate snake. It was a meal remembered for a long time. They dry the rest for jerky and snacks.

Janice and David's twin daughters, Rebecca and Renee are 18 years old. They help with gathering food items and making our menus for the week, which are posted at the entrance to our dining room, and community meeting area. We take our meals all together except for the man on duty/watch, a plate is taken to him.

Janice and David's oldest son Jerry 20 helps Martha 32 and Joseph 30 teach the younger children every day for a few hours. They teach basic lessons to all the children under 18 years old, which makes a class of five; Dale, Donna, Susan, Denise and Jesse our rebellious 16 year old going on 30 and then sometimes his older sister Lynn 19 sits in on the class, to help out and listen.

My brother Joseph also helps with the repair of things and building things that can be used to make our lives easier. He is very good with his hands and very handy in creating new gadgets.

Joseph is friends with all the single guys; most of them went to college together and decided to stay here.

Their families were in other cities and states. It was a hard decision for Stan and Matthew, but they decided it was for the best. I knew it would be a burden on their families and they had a better chance of survival here.

Aaron and I are fond of each other, we talk a lot together and he is cute. I think our doctor Sarah likes John too. Lynn told me she has a crush on Michael and Martha has an eye for my brother Joseph only because they spend time together planning school lessons each day. I have sat in on a couple of their classes and I have to admit they work well together. I notice the way Martha looks at him.

Days turn into weeks and weeks into months. Before we know it, it has been over a year and we are celebrating Halloween and we make customes for the kids and they hunt for candies and fruits. Another Thanksgiving we share together, and butcher three roosters with all the trimmings and have a wonderful evening and there are lots of prayers of thanksgiving for all we have. We become very close, like a big family. We have our troubles, problems and difficult decisions to make, as we continue to live and grow together in a confined place.

Our first Christmas and everyone pitches in to make decorations for the tree we keep in a box. We slaughter a male pig for the feast and really have a wonderful time. We sing carols and exchange small tokens and share memories until late. There is plenty of pork left over for many days to follow.

Happy New Year 2200 everyone, we all say together with a shared bottle of our precious champagne, used for only special occasions. We spend the evening reflecting on our year together.

One day in mid-March we all get some interesting, exciting and scary news. Depending on how you looked at it and who you were, of course.

"The three of us are planning to go out for a scouting mission. We will be needing, food, water, weapons, and a medical kit." Michael says to us at the dinner table the next night. Jason and Aaron nod with a smile. "John has approved this first mission, and we will stay in contact with our walkie-talkie radios. We mapped out a five-mile radius around our camp to see if there are others near by. We will be leaving in the morning." Michael shifts in his chair and glances over at John. "I think its time to scout out our territory and put markers of owner ship out for would be travelers or rebels. I don't want to scare anyone but we are not alone on this planet and there could be others who might want to attack, pillage, and take our food, weapons, women or even our home."

John looks around the large table. "I'm only being realistic and honest. We can not stay down here forever, and I know for a fact, there will be marauders to deal with sooner or later." John straightens his vest.

"You know just because you were in the military at

one time, don't think that everything is bad, evil or out to destroy us." David says rather loudly.

John puts his hand up, "I know David, but we have to think of our future, if we plan to grow and stay together as a unit. It has worked so far only because we have played it safe and we need each other to survive, but the time is to move on and things need to change and we need to change with it. If we don't start to make some moves forward we will fall apart or be taken over by more powerful groups. And I for one could not stand or handle that." John says standing and walking out.

Everyone seems upset and start talking all at once.

"Shhh! Quiet, please."

"I say lets all sleep on it and give our scouting party time to check things out and give us their reports, suggestions and findings." Leo says as he stands and takes Esther's hand to leave.

The rest of us try to discuss the possibilities and air our concerns.

An hour later, I find Sarah putting items into a small bag. "This is for the boys, give it to them and wish them luck for me, Rachel." She smiles and places it in my hands. "What do you think, Sarah?" I ask staring into her wise brown eyes.

"Well I think John is right, but it frightens me too. To stay here safe is wonderful, but for how long? We need to protect ourselves against anything that might come our way. So it is the right thing to do. We need to know what's out there be it friend or foe." She says squeezing my hand with a smile. I nod and leave to find Aaron.

"Hey!" I shout, when I see Aaron leaving the kitchen with supplies. I give him the medical kit. "You be careful out there and watch each others backs." I say giving him a hug.

"Thanks Rachel, I promise to come back because there is something I want to ask you." He kisses me softly on the lips and walks on to his sleeping area to finish packing. I stand alone, leaning against the rocks and say a silent prayer for his safe return.

Lynn and I have become close friends, she is a year younger than I am and her boy friend Michael is going too. I go looking for Lynn and find her with the lambs. She loves the animals, but hates it when we have to kill them for food. We have two cows for milk and one of the cows had a male calf. Two sheep and one ram, plus three lambs right now. So we also use the wool too, some of the ladies, spin and knit. A male and a female pig and she just had her second litter of nine piglets, which means we eat a lot of pork, but it's very good and fixed many different ways, plus we dry it for jerky.

I am not sure how many chickens, roosters and chicks. They are our main source of food and eggs, of course. They also help keep the insects down.

We stored an entire barn full of hay and grains for feed. They also get the greens from our garden to help with their diet.

Joseph, John and Stan built the water troth system that flows in from the pool and connects with the garden irrigation lines too.

We use the animal waste for the gardens and it works well. Nothing goes to waste, because everything is too precious.

"Lynn, do you have a few minutes to talk?" I ask as I pick up a little yellow chick.

"Sure, Rach, what's up? Let me guess, it's about the trip, huh?" I nod my head, yes. "I can't help feeling something bad is going to happen." Sighing I sit down on a boulder near by.

"Hey you, it's going to be all right, silly. Michael and Jason will look after him, besides Michael told me a secret and I know they will be back," Lynn giggles and gives me a reassuring hug. "Here, help me feed the animals." We talked some more while we fed all the animals and I felt better after our visit.

After leaving Lynn I go to the gardens to help my parents. "Hi mom, hi dad, can I help you?" Dad waves me over, his hands covered in mud. "Here, hold the hose, while I plant this new tree." He carefully takes it out of the big pot and puts it into the muddy hole, covering it with dirt and a little manure. I water it and smile up into his loving hazel eyes.

That nights dinner is pretty quiet, everyone with his or her own private thoughts about the future.

Aaron and I spend the evening near the pool holding hands and talking about our life together. "You promise to come back and take care of me, right?" I lean against his chest and he strokes my long dark chestnut hair.

"You know, I will be fine and we will be back soon, as I said before. I want to ask you something very important." He kisses my forehead and holds me tight as we talk a little more before he walks me back to my bed for the night.

Morning arrives and I spring out of bed, splashing water on my face and race to where Aaron sleeps. As I approach I see he is gone already. I run down to the entrance just in time to shout good-bye and throw him a kiss. Lynn is standing there crying and we hold each other as the large boulder rolls back across the entrance. It was the first time we had opened our door since coming down inside over a year ago and everyone was curious, but only the mission party ventured outside. The thick orange dust blows inside, as the men put on their masks and leave.

Lynn and I walked to the kitchen to get a drink in silence. Janice and her twins looked up as we walked in. "Hi you two." Rebecca and Renee say in unison. Janice smiles, "They will be back before you two know it. It's only a three-day mission. Here drink some freshly pressed tomato juice." We take the cups of juice and sit down on stools and watch them fix breakfast. They all do such a good job feeding us all and the menus are always varied.

The kitchen is full of cookbooks and every pot and pan you can think of. There are all sorts of silverware, cutlery and dishes too. There is even crystal stemware. We have a large rock area that is very cold and in the winter for storage we have been wrapping some meats and burying it in the snow, it seems to keep it very good. We can, stew, pickle, dry and candy everything we have, so it keeps, especially through the winter.

There is one long counter with a butcher-block type top. There are two large tubs for washing the dishes and the food for our meals. The tables are long picnic type tables with bench chairs. We have two rows of three tables each along the two opposite sides, so we keep a clear isle in the middle.

The day goes by slowly and I notice most of us preoccupied in deep thoughts, of what might be found on the outside, or if they run into any other people, or trouble. We all know the risk involved when they venture out beyond our protection. But we also realize we are not the only people who managed to live through the destruction of earth. But who knows what our group will run into.

We all say silent prayers for their safe return.

Chapter 2

"Hey! Aaron over here." Michael yells out. Aaron quickly makes his way over to a small hilltop. Jason is close on his heels.

All three of them stand on the top of the hill, gazing down into the valley below. It is barren and orange dirt covers everything. They had walked the five miles north and it was late in the afternoon.

"Nothing," Jason says sadly. "Nothing at all as far as the eye can see."

Michael nods and Aaron squats down picking up a hand full of dry brown earth. "Sad, I wonder if it will ever return?" Shaking his head, he glances up into the orange hued sky.

"Let's find a place to camp for the night. We can take off at first light, heading east, Okay?" Jason says as he puts in the ground a five mile green markers with claim number 100 of the Silver Haven's Community emblem. They use big silver SH letters on red paper.

Michael walks off toward the east and a group of

large boulders. "That sounds good to me." Aaron says as he follows Michael to set up camp and start a fire for their evening meal.

Jason returns and sits down unrolling his knapsack taking out his meager meal of dried snake and carrots.

The hazy sun disappeared to the west quickly and it turns cold and dark, except for the orange haze moonlight. No sounds, nothing but the crack of the fire. They all fall asleep with their private dreams.

Morning comes early to find Aaron stoking the ambers to make some tea to drink with their biscuits for breakfast. They pack up and head east. They walk along in silence taking in the terrain as they go, marking the map carefully.

As the sun rises high in the hazy sky, far to their left they hear a deep rumbling and take off at a run to investigate. The closer they get to the hillside the louder the sounds gets. They quicken their pace to see the earth being swallowed up into a deep gash in the ground and the hillside slowly sliding into it.

"The earth is so dried out it is cracking open and taking the mountain with it." Michael says loudly over the noise.

All of sudden Jason falls to his knees as blood sprays from his chest, and falls face down into the dirt. Michael and Aaron look up to see five armed men in black running toward them. They turn and quickly pick up Jason, running west as fast as they can toward the earth disturbance into the far side of the hill and climb up into the rocks and wait for their attackers.

Michael grabs all their rifles and loads and cocks them, then taking the three handguns slamming the clips into the nine millimeters. He turns to Jason now coughing up blood and opens the medical kit. He applies disinfectant and gives him a shot of morphine and puts a large compress on the wound.

"It looks bad, Jason. Hold on buddy." Michael turns to Aaron and tosses him Jason's handgun, he takes his rifle and they get ready for the rush.

They did not have long to wait, when two of the five come rushing up the hill towards them guns blazing.

Michael took aim and blew one of them right off his feet, as the other one dove for cover. The other three came up behind them cautiously and a gun battle resumed.

Again Michael takes his time and squeezes off another round hitting one guy in the shoulder. A bullet sings by Aaron's head and he stands up and empties his whole clip at them.

"Save your ammo Aaron." Michael yells as another bullet ricashays off the rocks. The rally continues for hours it seems, it's like a stand off. Jason has passed out, but Michael fears the worse.

"Hey!" Someone yells from below. "Let's call a truce and go our separate ways, what do you say?"

"Come out and show yourself with empty hands, since you started this mess." Michael yells back as they wait with guns poised.

Then suddenly from the corner of Aaron's eye he sees a shadow slowly moving up behind them. He goes down spinning around and with one-shot takes out the guy. He yells falling off the rocks and the others open fire again.

As the sun starts to go down things quiet, due to the fact they can't see anything, it has grown very dark, and cold.

They cover Jason with their blankets, but he doesn't look good. "He is going into shock, and I do not think he is going to make it, Aaron." Michael says softly taking Jason's pulse. "It's very weak. Keep your eyes peeled Aaron." As he tosses him a piece of dried snake jerky.

Aaron catches it and nods, taking a drink of water and chewing on the meat. He focuses on the rocks below as total darkness engulfs them and the temperature drops.

"No fires tonight," Michael says zipping up his jacket and pulling up the collar. "Stay alert Aaron," He say as he moves to sit next to Jason.

Aaron gives him a salute, "no problem here, what do we do next Michael?" He shakes his head, "don't know buddy, let's see what tomorrow brings." Michael turns back to Jason as Aaron continues to watch into the night.

Morning comes and Aaron glances at Michael leaning over Jason. He pulls his jacket over Jason's face and crosses himself. "We lost him during the night… Damn it!"

Aaron moves over to them, "shit," he stands up and takes two handguns running down the hill, both guns blasting, only to find one dead man and one dying. "Hey, Michael they pulled out, come on down." Aaron yells, as he stares at the wounded man.

Michael runs down the hill to see Aaron standing over the dying man. "What is your name, and where is your camp?" Aaron shouts, kicking the man's leg.

"Ack, please, stop." He says coughing. "He took one bullet in the shoulder and one in the stomach, Aaron." Michael says leaning down examining him.

"Where is your camp from here?" Aaron asks again, cocking his gun. "About three days north of where we first picked up your tracks." He coughs again holding his belly.

"How many of you are there?" Aaron asks squatting down closer. "There is about 90 of us, all men from the stone prison. We are running out of food fast. We have been out on patrols for some time now." He says rolling and groaning on the ground.

"Holy shit!" Michael shouts, "This is not good, not good at all. We need to get back and warn the others quick."

"Well, we killed three of them, and that's good odds I'd say." Aaron says with a smile. "Three?" Michael questions.

"Yes, because this poor guy isn't going to make it."

They both turn and walk back up the hill to get their gear. They decide to bury Jason there, instead of carrying him back to camp. "Bless his soul and please watch over us, at least until we get back to camp."

Michael says, crossing himself again. He pats the dirt down and says a silent prayer.

"No marker, Aaron says as he picks up Jason's coat and gear. "Come on, Michael. Let's get a move on." Michael nods, picking up all the rest of the supplies and gear. They go back down the hill, heading west.

"Hey, your not going to leave me here are you?" The dying man says pleadingly. "Your so called friends did, why should we be any different?" Aaron says angrily. "Besides you killed our buddy." Michael continues to walk on slowly.

"Come on man, give me a break, I' m bleeding here." He shouts at them. Aaron turns around and walks right up to him and puts one shot into his head. Michael jumps at the sharp pop, but keeps walking, not turning back. Aaron takes another minute to quickly go through the man's belongings, taking anything of use or value. He runs to catch up with the still walking Michael.

They walk in silence until nightfall. They camp with no fire that night and few words are spoken between them.

At dawn they were on the move again and by evening they gave the password, "Mother Earth," to enter the encampment. "Where's Jason?" Matthew asks as Michael and Aaron are allowed inside. "He's dead, we were attacked." Michael whispers. "Oh my god!" Matthew says wide-eyed. "Everyone is going into dinner, you better go tell them at once." Matthew waves them through and glancing outside quickly and closes the entrance tight.

They both walk straight into the dining area where Sarah just finished saying grace. Everyone turns and looks up toward the door as they walk in. Lynn and I jump up and run to their side.

They drop everything right where they stand, and Aaron shouts, "We were attacked and Jason was killed!" He goes down on one knee. Everyone gathers around them to hear all the details.

"There are about 90 men from an old prison in the hills up north, John. To many for us, we need to come up with a plan." Michael says. Lynn brings him a drink of water, while I hold Aaron's hand, shaking.

"Tell us everything you two can remember about them, don't leave out one thing." John says as Sarah attends to their cuts and bruises. John takes notes while he listens to every detail.

After the excitement settles down and Aaron and Michael have a chance to eat and bath, John calls a meeting, we all are in attendance.

"Let's discuss a plan of action and defense of what will happen sooner or later." John says as he sits down.

"I told you, didn't I. Now see what has happened, Jason is dead and you have put us all in jeopardy." David shouts out angrily.

"Calm yourself, David." John says putting up his hands. "We need to decide how to fortify our home. The entrance is very well hidden, they would have to really be looking close and they can't get inside from outside, so we are pretty secure." Daniel says walking around with his hands behind his back.

"The guy said they were about ten miles away from us, so it's safe to say, that it has taken them this long to get this far, let alone to find our entrance. I'd say we are pretty safe." Aaron says in a reassuring manner.

"Besides, there is no reason to go outside again for a long time. We were just curious and a little stir crazy. But at least we know there are other people out there and not very friendly either." Michael says nodding to Aaron. Everyone nods agreement.

"I am scared," Rebecca and Renee say in unison. "It's Okay girls." Their father David says softly, "as long as we stay down here hidden, we will be fine, don't worry. No one will find us."

"True enough, David." Damien says, "But I for one need to know more of what's happening out there and what we are up against."

"So do I," Daniel says standing up putting a hand on his brother's shoulder. "That's why are leaving together to scout out this threat and find their weaknesses or start taking them out one by one. They started it and we intend to finish it." Both boys nod and stand their ground.

Brett the quiet one walks over to them and says, "I plan on going along too, so they stay out of trouble."

"Ok, now it's the three musketeers!" Sarah says with a smile walking off toward the pool.

"Well, we need to get ready. Let's make up a list of things we need and our plan of operation." Brett says smiling to the brothers as he walks off toward his sleeping quarters to pack. Brett comes from a long line of government men, so he is very organized and logical.

The three of them talk until everyone has gone to bed about their trip, mapping out their area, with the help of Michael and Aaron. "Five miles north of here is where the guy said they picked up our tracks, so I got the feeling they were still north from there, because of the heavy jackets and the direction we first spotted them. We could come with you, want us too?" Michael says taking a deep breath.

"Thanks, but you need to stay here and take care of your girls and the rest of things, besides you might be needed here Michael, you too Aaron." Damien says with a nod from his brother.

Aaron points to a place on the map saying, "They came over this ridge from the northwest, so be on your guard once you get to this point."

"Good night," Michael says waving. "See you off in the morning." Aaron takes the cue and stands and follows Michael out to leave them alone to finish up the details.

They all go to sleep that night thinking about all the news they received, about the danger outside. Their dreams wake a few and interest others as the night turns into day.

Chapter 3

Morning comes and Daniel, Damien and Brett are packing up their final items for the mission. They layer their clothes; pack a bedroll and personal items.

Sarah brings them another medical kit, and their masks. They go to the kitchen for water and food supplies and then finally off to the weapons locker.

"I want a shot gun and 12 gauge buckshot, a nine millimeter with two full clips and two boxes of shells and a combat knife." Brett says loading up his gear.

"We will each take a rifle, a handgun and a knife." The brothers say together, smiling at Brett, who looks like Rambo. They load up their gear and head for the entrance. Everyone is there to wish the men well and a safe journey.

"Keep a log and map it all out for us on your return, so we have a feel for the area to our north." John says firmly. "Watch your sixes, boys. See you back here in one piece, with lots of information to report real soon." We all wave as the entrance boulder is rolled to one side. We squeeze toward the opening and watch them disappear over the rise, as the door closes tightly.

"I hope they make it back and find what they seek." My mother Esther says softly as she and father walk back to the garden with Leah.

We all return to our duties and routines of every day life. We all say prayers, for our brave boys, the mission and their return.

The threesome makes it to the five-mile marker to the north by mid-day. Brett uses the binoculars to look out to the north from a small hill. He takes his time scanning the area slowly moving west then due east. Far off to the northeast he catches a reflection or glimmer from metal or perhaps a mirror, he drops down to the ground quickly. He motions for Daniel and Damien to come up low and he whispers. "I got sight of a flash from either a gun or binoculars far off to the northeast on the next large hill top, maybe a days fast pace, but the bad news is that it is all open ground. We would be sitting ducks during the day-light." Brett says taking out the map and marking it, noting the time, distant and makes a comment of a possible encounter.

"Hey, do you guys remember the name of the prison near Diamond Bluff." Daniel asks looking at them thinking.

"Huh, yeah, I think, wasn't it Highett Penitentiary? Or something like that." Damien says. "Yeah!, some mighty bad boys up there too." Damien says, "That's not good news."

"I know," agrees Brett. "Let's wait until dark then

make a run for the far hill side, Okay?" Brett asks looking at the brothers. They agree and settle down to eat, drink and rest up for the race.

As the sun begins to set, they get ready. They strip down to only black clothes and carry only handguns and knifes. They mix some water in the dirt and smear it all over their hands and face. Then slowly make it down to the bottom of the small hill and make ready for the race across the open plain to the opposite hillside.

They take off running flat out until they tier and then a fast pace walk. Its pitch black by the time they make it to the foothills of the opposite rise. Then very slowly and quietly inch their way up to the top of the hill.

Down on the opposite side is what they were looking for, there are lights coming from a dark structure in the side of the mountain.

Suddenly they hear gravel shifting, and they quickly hug the ground, and wait for the approach. Two men come into view armed, dressed in black. They are talking and one is smoking a cigarette. Brett waits until they walk by and motions Daniel and Damien.

They both jump up quickly from behind the men and Daniel snaps one neck, while Damien runs his knife across the throat of the other man. They didn't know what hit them. It was done like professionals, quick, quiet and deadly.

They drag the bodies off into the rocks, removing their coats and weapons. Then stack rocks over them and continue down the hill very slowly, listening to every sound, eyes piercing the black night. They focus on the floodlights from the now large gray looming building in front of them. They wait a moment longer and listen.

"Shhh!" Brett signals them down, hugging the rocks. Two more men come out of a tunnel, laughing and smoking. They walk right past Brett and he nods to the brothers.

Again in unison they take out the two unsuspecting men, this time they take the best weapons and stash everything else along with the two dead bodies under some near by rocks.

They are invisible against the dark gray rocks in the black night as they crawl over to the tunnel entrance. Taking a moment to listen, Brett goes in first. They move at arms length, backs flat up against the stone tunnel wall, inching there way further and further inside.

There is chatter up a head, Brett motions to stop, holding up his fist and cupping his ears to the brothers. Three men start walking toward them; they all take a left at the junction.

Brett sucks in a breath, nodding to the brothers.

They quicken their pace silently up behind the three men and in unison knifes slice across their throats. They drag the three bodies back outside and bury them with their two mates.

Sliding back inside Brett puts up seven fingers then a thumb down. The two brothers nod as they continue once again on their investigation and killing spree. They make it back to where they were and stop at the junction.

"Straight left or right? All three ways are lit. Let's split up and meet back here in ten minutes." Brett says adjusting his watch. "Okay!" they all agree and take off cautiously.

In ten minutes Brett is back waiting for the brothers in the shadows. Damien comes back next, one finger up and a thumb down. Daniel comes back slowly holding his side. "He got me before I could finish him off." Dan drops to his knees.

Brett and Damien quickly pick him up and carry him outside the tunnel. Brett opens the medical kit and pulls out a bottle of pills, popping two into Dan's mouth. Opening his shirt he pours disinfectant into the knife wound and wraps him tightly. "It's not too bad, I cleaned it up and it should be all right for now. Dan, I want you to crawl up into those rocks and shoot anyone coming out, except us, of course." Brett chuckles, then hands Dan the bottle of painkillers. "There were only more tunnels my way," Dan says taking two rifles and all the guns from the dead guys.

"Find yourself a good place to see the entrance and stay well hidden. "Okay," Dan says as he slowly makes his way back up into the hills. Brett watches him disappear, "He will be fine, don't worry, Damien." He nods his head, "I know it's us I am worried about." He grins, "Hey, there are sleeping quarters my way."

"Good lets go, there was only kitchen and dining area mine." Brett says, as Damien leads the way back to where he found most of them sleeping in their cells.

One by one Brett and Damien slaughter the prison

mates sleeping, and unaware of the dangerous dreams.

Brett flashes 10-20-30-2 fingers up in the now bloody face of Damien; he nods with a grin of understanding. The two of them continue their gruesome task until they reach the end of the cell-block with locked gates. They turn and slowly make their way back to the junction.

Suddenly out of the shadows two men jump them. Knocking them to the floor, they fight and struggle. One of them calls out for help, as Damien guts him, then pulling his handgun he rolls over and shoots the other one in the head, who has Brett pinned down.

POP! It echo's through the tunnels, Damien helps Brett to his feet and they sprint out of the tunnel, yelling, "Hold your fire, Dan, were coming out." They run straight toward the mountainside.

Its now early dawn and suddenly machine-gun fire rings out over the rocks, and the bullets start flying everywhere.

Brett takes a round in the arm. "Shit!" He drops to the ground spread eagle. Daniel reaches out and drags him by the jacket collar to the safety of the rocks. Damien pulls them both out of the way of flying bullets.

They all crawl up the rocks to higher ground and out of the range of the towers guns.

"We took out 39 of them." Brett gasps tying a strip of his shirt around his upper arm. Damien quickly checks Daniels side wound, and it is bleeding again.

He opens the medical kit and tosses Brett some pills and applies a powder on Dan's cut, wrapping it tightly again with clean bandages, he hands him another pill too.

"Let's lock and load boys, I think we are in for a war." Damien says, as the rally of bullets from the tower stops, when they finally realize there out of range.

There is a loud machine motor noise, then in moments a large metal doors open upward from the structure and a huge armored truck rolls out. Guns blazing in all directions, with nine guys in body armor running behind it with assault rifles.

The three boys fortify themselves with all the weapons they have, take a drink of water and wait for them to come closer. Damien lights a cigar and smiles. He pulls three sticks of dynamite out of his vest jacket, lighting one he gives it a good throw. It lands right on top of the gunner in the truck, blowing him and the gun to bits.

"YES!" Damien shouts, throwing another stick into the scattering foot soldiers, three go flying. Brett leans up on a rock and sends a rally of rifle fire at the men racing for cover. Daniel holds his side and rolls in between a narrow path with rocks on either side of him and waits. The truck can't make it up the rocky incline so the three inside climb out, only to be picked off one by one, all three are shot down.

"Yes!" Brett shouts. Damien lets another stick of TNT fly. Everyone holds their breath waiting to see where it lands.

"Bingo!" Damien claps his hands, as it drops on top of the truck, blowing out the front window and the hood of the truck goes flying, with a flaming whirl. The remaining men with the truck high tail it back to the compound, as Brett opens fire once again and only two make it back inside and to safety.

"Let's regroup and get back to Silver Haven, its going to take a good full two days with us helping Daniel." Brett says holding his arm. Damien wipes blood from his eyes. "It's only a graze, I'm fine, it's nothing, let's go." Damien picks up his brother and they head south toward home. Brett carries as much of the supplies and weapons as he can, as night falls once more.

They walk until they can't see any more and the three exhausted warriors make camp behind a small mound.

Daniel has passed out and Brett's arm aches from carrying everything. Damien quickly opens Dan's dressing to check it. He cleans it and rewraps it. "The bleeding has stopped and it looks pretty good. How are you doing?" Damien asks looking at Brett.

"I'll be alright, here I saved this for Dan." Brett says popping a pill and handing him the only syringe of painkiller.

Damien puts it into his jacket and pulls out some dried meat and carrots. They eat and then get some sleep.

Morning finds Daniel holding his side drinking water, while Brett still sleeps. Dan gives Damien a kick in the feet. "Hey, I'm dying here, is there anything left for the pain?"

Damien nods, "Brett saved it for you," giving him the shot.

Dan starts to relax and eats a biscuit and drinks more water. Brett leans over and grabs the canteen, "Hey, take it easy on the water, that one and mine are all we have left."

"Okay, sorry." Dan takes a deep breath, "Come on let's get going, we have a very long days journey ahead of us."

Damien helps Dan to his feet and he walks for a while, until the pain gets too much for him. Damien helps him again. Brett carries everything again, putting a carrot in Damien's mouth and giving Dan another drink, they continue their homeward trek.

It's pitch black outside, by the time they finally crawl back to the entrance, and give the password. "Mother Earth." Brett shouts at the boulder. It takes a few moments until the boulder slowly rolls open.

Stan has his rifle poised with eyes wide open. "Jesus, you guys look like hell." The three stagger inside as Daniel falls to the ground, Brett yells, "Go get Sarah, now!" Stan takes off like a shot.

Damien closes the entrance and drops to his knees. Brett opens Dan's jacket to see he is bleeding again, "looks like he is going to need stitches." Brett says pressing a clean cloth on his side. "Here," Damien tosses him the canteen. They finish the water and wait for Sarah. Brett is very pleased with their mission.

Sarah comes rushing over with another medical kit, kneeling down beside Daniel. She gives him a shot of morphine and one to Brett. She looks back at Dan with some concern, "he has lost a lot of blood, Damien how are you feeling?"

"I have a bad headache, a little achy but all right I guess, why?" He says as he stares at his brother. She re-wraps Dan's wound, can you carry him to his bed?" Damien nods and picks his brother up. "I will be there in a few minutes. I need to get my other kit. You lay down too." She leaves in a hurry, Brett leaves everything at the entrance as Jerry and Matthew come over and take care of it all. They check out the new assault rifles and commando knifes.

Soon Sarah arrives at the bed of Daniel. "Move your bed over here Damien and lay down with your arm out." He does as she orders without a word, when he realizes what she is going to do.

"Your brother needs a blood transfusion or he will not survive." He nods and lies down in silence, rolling up his shirt.

Sarah attaches the tubes and needles and lets it run for a time. She then turns to Brett; she motions for him to sit down. Un-wrapping his arm, she examines it. "The bullet went right through, you'll be fine." She cleans and packs the wound, wraps it and gives him some more oral meds.

"Thanks," he sighs and lies down and watches his friends. She turns back to Daniel's arm to check for any reaction. He is sleeping peacefully.

Later Brett and Damien go and wash up and find

John in the dining room with the other men, they go over the map and inform them of their entire mission.

"We took a lot of them out, it was a little touch and go there for a while. But we made them run. It was such an adrenal rush." Brett says with pride and excitement in his voice, "you should have been there John."

"Oh and by the way the walkie-talkies are useless with this orange fall out and all the mountain area, I think." Damien says. "So it will be one less thing for us to carry with us next time." He says again with a smile and a nod.

John smiles, "I think your right, but you guys did a great job, I'm proud of you all." The men go over every detail of the mission and talk of the adventure before turning in for a much-deserved sleep.

The future safety of their home is now becoming an issue, they cannot ignore. It is getting to close for comfort and something needs to be done to rid them of the threat to their way of life.

CHAPTER 4

Another morning and everyone is in the dining room eating breakfast. "I would like to make an announcement," Aaron says standing up. He takes my hand and pulls me to him. "Rachel and I are engaged and plan to marry in the spring."

Everyone claps and cheers. I glance at my mother, moist wide eyes and she smiles. My dad comes over and pats Aaron on the back. "Take care of my little girl, son." He smiles and gives me a hug.

Aaron and I stay in the dining room and plan our wedding. "Let's have Lynn and Michael, be our best man and maid of honor. My dad gives me away and then we can have a big party, the first wedding in Silver Haven." I say smiling up at Aaron.

"It's what ever you want, my sweet Rachel." He says kissing my cheek.

Things fall back into the routine of life around camp. Brett's arm is getting better and thanks to Damien's blood his brother is recovering slowly, but nicely.

Everyone is busy with projects and tasks of day-to-day life, keeping active, and trying not to think of the troubles or danger, all except John. He has been drawing the camps area's, in's and out's, taking inventory of all supplies and weapon's. Sarah has been counting the medical supplies, especially the drugs that have been used up lately. She worries about any major battle and if she can handle it. Jane and Sam have control on the livestock and it seems to be holding its own, fresh grass would be nice, but of course, that is out of the question, there is no such thing any more. The animals do get all the vegetable stocks, leafs and waste from the garden, so it helps a little. Plus there are vitamin supplements for the animals too.

Sam helps John with the weapons, since the addition of the new weapons of the recent raid. Mom and Dad keep a close eye on our garden. The fruits and vegetables are growing well and doing great. Janice, David and the twins are in the kitchen preparing the Sunday dinner, which is always a meat dish. Tonight is chicken or rooster, actually. Twenty-seven people eat three roosters with potatoes and peas with bread and butter. Dinner is the main meal; it's usually about five o'clock each evening. Breakfast is about seven in the morning. Food supplies are holding up well. Water is not a problem, but our gasoline is running low. Keeping things warm in winter and our fires for the cooking and some lights, however, we still have lots of batteries but they too need to be recharged from time-to-time. All in all everything is pretty good, considering we have been on our own for almost two years now, with no outside help or intrusion.

"Help! Help! Someone help me." Comes the shouts of Lynn carrying in Denise. She had bites all over her hands, feet and face. "Its rats I think, I found her laying in the west tunnel." Lynn says as she lays Denise down gently on Sarah's cot. Sarah examines Denise carefully and notices the swollen, and infected bites. "It appears that she has been bitten a lot, and not just this time, there are healed bites too. She looks like she has lost some blood too, by her pale pallor, and a fever as well," Sarah says, taking her temperature. "Lynn go get John, and her mother please." Lynn nods and runs off in search of John and Jane.

Moments later John shows up looking concern with what Lynn had told him on the way to Sarah.

"John, I think we have a major rat problem, perhaps due to ridding the camp of all the snakes. We need to do something soon, or there could be a serious health risk for all of us."

John understands and calls an emergency meeting. "We have a rat problem, boys and girls. I need volunteers to go into the tunnels and seek out these pests and destroy them. They are starting to attack the children and we need to stop them as soon as we can before they get totally out of control." John looks around at everyone and he gets nods from the group. "Let's get, bags, knives, shoves, and clubs. We kill them and put them into the bags for disposal outside. Understood?"

Everyone starts off to different parts of the encampment, equipped with what they need to rid themselves of the vermin that has invaded our home.

Jane spends the entire day with her daughter. "I thought she was getting pale, but I thought maybe she was coming down with a cold. Then she complained of feeling tired and I notices a few bites, but I thought they were just bug bites she had been scratching. I'm so sorry, Denise", she starts to cry and Sarah comforts her and assures her she will be all right. "Let's have a look at Donna and Dale too. Or anyone else that has found some bites on them." Sarah orders and mixes a drink for Denise.

Things get very busy with the rat hunt and the boys are having a blast on their killing spree. There are six bloody bags brought to the entrance by the end of the day. "Man, there was an entire shaft full of them. It was like a sea of rats, it was disgusting. But I think we got them all, I need a bath." Matthew says wiping his bloody hand over his forehead.

The boys decide to join in a community swim and bath together. They got a ball and started a game of water volleyball. They were having a good time after the bloody ordeal of the hunt. They all deserved it, for it was not a nice job, but it had to be done.

Mid-spring and there is excitement in the air. Sarah will marry us right after Sunday services and Mom, Leah, Lynn and I have been behind a curtain getting ready. Mom pulls out a large cedar chest and opens it. The smell is wonderful. She lifts a long beautiful white wedding dress out, and a box with a matching veil and shoes. It was her mother's before. Lynn squeals with joy at the sight of the lovely dress. Leah was mesmerized by the pearls and glittering beads.

They helped me into it and it fit perfectly. Mom arranged the headpiece and the six-foot train. The shoes of white satin were a little too big, but mom stuffed tissue in the toes and they were fine. Everyone is gathered in the dining room, with the long table and chairs moved to one side.

They are all waiting for us now. I get so nervous that my knees start to shake and my mom kisses my cheek and gives me a hug.

"You look so beautiful, Rachel. I am so proud of you, I love you so much." Mom smiles and wipes her eyes. Lynn and Michael walk in first as I wait by the door, trying to steady myself. Dad grips my arm and winks. Martha sings, "Here comes the bride."

As we slowly walk down the middle of the large room. She sings lovely and we stop in front of Sarah. My dad gives my arm to Aaron and Martha finishes the song as Sarah starts the ceremony. "This joining is the first for, Silver Haven and we welcome this new couple into our fold. Let's pray." We exchange the standard wedding vows and Mom gave Aaron my grand mothers ring. "I now pronounce you Husband and Wife, you may kiss your bride. May you live long and have many children. God Bless." Sarah smiles with a nod, as we turn and face everyone.

Everyone starts to clap and cheer as we kiss and hug each other and then greet everyone else with hugs and kisses. We dance as Stan plays the guaitar, and Martha sings. We eat cake; drink champagne that we save for special occasions. We received a few homemade items and everyone has a great time, except Matthew, it was his guard duty. So as the party continued we formed a Congo line and took Matt a plate of food and a drink.

"Congratulations, you two." Matt tips his glass to us and drinks it down with an appreciative smile. From there everyone goes back to his or her tasks and Aaron and I move our beds to a small alcove we scouted out the day before.

I changed and give the gown back to Mom, and then I pack up all my belongings and moved them to our new home together. I started setting things up as Aaron comes up behind me and hugs me tightly.

"You have made me the happiest man on earth, Rachel, my wife." He kisses my neck, my shoulder and turns me around and we kiss for a long time. He starts to explore my parted lips with his tongue and he lets his hands wander over my body.

My knees quiver as he pulls my sweater off and unfastens my bra. My full breasts bounce forth to his waiting hands, he cups them firmly and leans down and kisses them. I sigh deeply, as I pull off his shirt, kissing his chest. We lie down on our joined beds and fondle and explore each other for the first time as a newly married couple. We take our time making love, getting to know every inch of our bodies, smells, marks and curves. We try different positions and finally he rolls me to my back and slowly enters me for the first time.

I cry out at the first full penetration, as he gasps. I

hold him tightly as he begins the slow strokes of pleasure inside me. I meet him as I arch my back and we move in unison.

The pleasure soon catches me and I soar on the wings of a dove, the waves of passion carry me away as I moan out my desire into his ear, sucking his ear lobe. I feel him tighten about me as he builds up for a final thrust. He explodes his pent up desire and lust into my fertile vessel. We lay back in each other's arms for a long time.

"I love you so much, Rachel, and I will all ways take care of you." We kiss deeply, "I love you too, my sweet husband." We make love throughout the night, drifting off to sleep and dreaming of our future. As dawn approaches Aaron is kissing my back caressing my breast and sliding easily into my wetness and within a few strokes he is releasing his seed into me once more. We drift back to sleep in spoon fashion and I smile at the warm, loving, secure feeling I have inside. We wake to the sound of people stirring about the business of the day and decide to go down to the pool to bath.

Lynn and Michael have just finished their bathing. We wave and begin our daily routines. "See you later Aaron. I need to help in the garden today." Aaron waves and blows me a kiss good-bye. Mom and Dad are already picking peas and tomatoes when I arrive.

"Good morning, married lady." Dad says as mom chuckles. "We are making a big salad for dinner tonight with spaghetti, so pick a lot of vegetables. "Okay," I say grabbing a basket and clippers.

"All right, class let's start our test, open your books and begin, now." Martha says as she takes Denise on her lap to read a story.

My brother Joseph is with Jerry and they are creating some exercise equipment from all the old parts stored in the back.

Everyone is busy doing their jobs; making things ready just encase its needed. The following evening John announces that he, Damien, Brett and Daniel are all going out on mission three to our south this time.

"We will be leaving in a couple of days and will be gone three or four days. We will start packing up supplies tonight and leave soon." John says as the group all walk out together talking about tomorrow. The rest of us sit and chat for a while and clean up before getting into our personal night modes.

Each of us has our own ideas about the missions and we know the dangers involved each time they go out, but for the most part we all know it is necessary for our survival.

Suddenly early the next morning the entire encampment starts to shake violently. The tunnel candles begin to fall off their stands attached to the walls. The animals become very nervous and noisy. The pool of water begins to splash out to the ground and one of the support beams near the pool breaks loose and falls hitting the pipes connecting the irrigation system. The water begins to rush through the tunnels.

Everyone scrambles to do their part in protecting what they can plus gathering up all the children to ensure their safety.

The trembling lasts for some time and before long there is a flood to deal with. The men rush up to the pool and quickly begin to repair the damaged pipeline. The water is cold and it takes four of the men to work together to finally get the pipes reattached. It takes the entire day to repair, but by evening things quiet down and people start to take inventory of the rest of the surrounding area inside and the clean up.

John and Brett go outside to survey the area and notice the hillside across from the entrance had been swallowed up into a large ravine. The entire landscape changed right before their eyes. It was disquieting and somewhat unnerving due to the fact it was just a short distance from their home.

They decided that things were safe now and went back inside to help clean up the mess and reset all the pipes.

Sarah and Martha got the children started on the candle replacement in all the tunnels with the help of the twins. It took two days to complete all the tunnels with resetting and lighting of all the candles. But as usual the kids made a game of it and before they knew it they were finished.

The earthquake had put a respect back into their home and at dinner that night, Sarah says a special prayer for their continued safety and a special thank you to god that no one was hurt or lost. It was a quiet night for everyone was exhausted from the ordeal.

But life goes on and the next patrol was around the corner.

CHAPTER 5

The mission was put off for a week but as the men were eager to be out exploring again they didn't delay much long.

As dawn comes on another new week some of us are up early to see mission three off. The four men are packed up and at the entrance ready to leave when Sarah rushes up and gives John a medical kit. "Try not to use it this time, OK?" She smiles and John gives her a hug.

"Will do boss, see you in a few days, keep a candle burning." Michael rolls the boulder open and the foursome takes off on their journey south.

They walk all morning going due south, stopping occasionally to mark the map and put marker down. "There is a ridge we can make by dusk, lets camp there." John says as he picks up the pace and by dark they are at the foothills of the ridge. They wander up the ridge until it becomes too dark to see. They decide to set up camp between some large boulders. Damien starts a fire and makes tea, warming their evening meal. They settle in for the night and get some much needed rest.

The next morning is bright and Brett looks up into the sky, "I wish there were birds singing, I sure miss that."

Stoking the fire, Damien smiles, "I know what you mean, I miss dogs barking and the smell of coffee."

Daniel laughs, "I sure don't miss traffic or the sound of alarms and sirens."

John laughs at their comments, "I miss everything and nothing." John says rolling up his bed, and taking the proffered cup of tea. "We should reach the top of the ridge by noon, if we leave now." They nod and pack up quickly. Damien buries the fire and hands everyone a stick of jerky. They hike up the ridge in a zigzag line. Finally they make it to the top at high noon.

John looks in all directions very slowly and calls out things to Brett, who is writing them down on the map. Dan and Damien sit and take a breather, before heading down the opposite side.

"Over to the south from here is a valley, to the east, mountains, west plains and north hills. Wait, just a minute I think I see a building or something southwest from here with some type of reflection. Let's go check it out." John says as he drops the binoculars and they swing around his neck, as he makes his way down the ridge in the direction of the structure. The three follow suit and soon are across the valley. The land is baron and lifeless.

By nightfall they are at the old abandon building, a warehouse of some type. Made of brown brick, concrete and a reddish paint, with lots of windows. "Before it gets too dark let's look around." John says breaking out his flashlight. They find the entrance barred and break off the lock easily. Caution high, they go inside with all four flashlights piercing the dark interior.

"John lets wait for day light, its too dangerous wandering around in here. I can't see much." Daniel says at the back of the group.

"Good idea Dan." Damien says as he turns around and back tracks outside.

"OK, but at first light we explore the place." John says, as Brett follows them all out, kicking a can of empty baked beans. "Looks like there had been people staying here for quite awhile."

"Yeah, I got that feeling too." John says making it toward the front door.

They set up camp, eat and sleep. Waking at dawn. John is eager to explore the building and leaves everything at the camp except his gun, flashlight and canteen.

"Hey, wait for me, John." Brett calls after him, running to catch up. In a few minutes all four are back inside. There is light filtering in through the door, broken windows, and cracks in the walls make it easier to see. They save their flashlights for later. Damien chews on some jerky and passes some around.

"Stay together, don't go wandering off to far." John

instructs them. "There are stairs leading up and down, let's break up into pairs and take the stairs."

"Okay, come with me Daniel. Brett you go with Damien." They all nod, John and Dan go upstairs and Damien and Brett take the down stairs. Brett takes the lead and quickly goes down the stairs, turning on his flashlight. Damien has his gun in one hand, flashlight in the other. It's a long flight of stairs that ends at a large metal door, marked employees only. Brett pushes on the door and surprisingly it opens with a creak. Brett now has his gun out too, as they walk in slowly, flashing the lights around in all directions.

"Looks like a meeting room or training room, with all the chairs, tables and white boards." Damien says, walking toward the opposite side of the room to another door. This door also opens easily. They go into a storage area there is moving items, boxes, cartons and other equipment and tools.

Suddenly one of the stacks of boxes falls over toward them.

"Look out!" They leap out of the way, just in time. "What the hell was that?" "I don't know. I didn't see anything." Brett says looking around carefully. "Be careful Brett." Damien says getting up and cocking his gun. They move slower through the rows of boxes. They both think they hear something.

They finally come to another door. Opening it slowly they see a sofa, chairs and tables. On one wall are vending machines, all have been broken open, its contents all gone. "It looks like an employee lounge or lunch room?" Brett says as he kicks candy wrappers.

"Yeah," Damien says, "it's a real mess in here." Then he looks up to a scurry sound above them. Both of their light beams hit a rat, running across the light fixtures hanging from the ceiling.

"There seems to be no shortage of rats in this place, watch it. There might be other animals or insects in here too."

"Huh, there appears to be some life here, watch your step" Brett says pushing on yet another door. "This is just the rest room. Nothing left in here either and by the smell of it, well used." Brett backs out holding his nose, "let's try the hall out to the right."

Damien heads for the door. They wander slowly out a dark hall, through double swinging doors to another storage area; in the distance is light streaming in. "Looks like a loading dock." Brett says and quickens his pace in that direction.

"Yeah, your right, it's going out to the long concrete dock that leads to a truck, half full of boxes." Damien opens one of the boxes, "computer parts." He chuckles, "useless." "There is another door over here. Lets take a look before heading back." Brett says moving to the left, down three steps to another metal door. He opens it with no problem. There is a shadow of movement that jumps across his eyes for a moment but he thinks it's just his eyes focusing. Then he hears something. Brett motions Damien that he saw and heard something. Damien crouches down and backs up to Brett as they go down the stairs into what looks like a basement or boiler room. Brett opens a door quickly and jumps back startled as a broom falls out, hitting him in the chest. "Shit!"

Damien chuckles, "this place gives me the creeps." Brett smirks, "I know what you mean."

Damien goes to another door and opens it quickly, stepping gingerly to one side. Flashing his light inside. "Brett, come here, looks like a sleeping area." Damien looks through the blankets, clothing, a doll and many empty cans and candy wrappers.

There are some pictures of a family, man, woman, a little boy and girl. There is another door to the right, but it's locked. "Huh, Brett, this is the first door we have found locked, except the entrance. Shall we?" Brett motions go for it, and Damien slams his shoulder into the door. Boom, the sound echoes throughout the basement, but the door holds. "Ouch!"

"Okay, I'll help this time." They both put their shoulders into it again. The door gives way this time. "Looks like another sleeping area." Damien says and catches sight of movement in the corner. Both their lights fall on a young man and girl huddled together. He has a knife poised at them in a defensive position.

"We will not hurt you, do you understand?" Brett says in a quiet slow tone. The girl nods her head, but the boy holds her back.

"They look half starved." Damien hands Brett some jerky, "here give them this." Brett reaches out with it and the girl snatches it up quickly, chewing it up in no time. Brett offers one to the boy and he slowly reaches for it. Brett tosses them his canteen and the girl gulps it down like she was dying of thirst. She finally hands it to her friend, or brother. He empties it and hands it back carefully.

"Do you understand me? Do you want to come with us?" Brett asks the girl, she nods her head and starts to stand. She is wearing tattered jeans and a shirt. She is about five feet tall ninety pounds if that, and by the looks and smell has not had a bath in a very long time.

The boy puts up a protective hand but she pushes it away and walks past him. "Tiff," the boy shouts as he springs up. "Stop, there dangerous, you remember, what mom and dad said." She turns back to him; her long matted red hair tumbles down her back, like a lion's mane.

"Then you stay, but I am tired of living like an animal and there is no food left, you can eat the rats if you want, but I for one want real normal food and fresh clean water." She turns back and takes Damien's hand by surprise. "Is there anyone else here?" Brett asks the boy.

"His name is Toby and he is my brother. I am Tiffany and we are twins. Mom and Dad I fear are dead. They left three weeks ago to find food and never returned." She starts to cry.

"Come on you two, let's get out of here. We need to meet up with the rest of our party." Brett says heading back out toward the far door and up the stairs. Toby gathers up his clothes, puts on a pair of old boots and follows them out. Tiffany grabs the pictures, her shoes, and doll, never letting go of Damien's hand. The four of them make there way back through the way they came and up the long staircase to where

John and Dan are waiting. They both jump up together as they see the two children following Brett and Damien.

"What do we have here?" John asks kneeling down looking at the two carrot tops. "This is Toby and his twin sister Tiffany. They have been here for what appears to be a long time. Damien says as Tiff nods her head in agreement. "I think Mom and Dad are dead." She says sadly. "Don't keep saying that Tiff, they just got lost or something." Toby snaps.

"Well, I'll bet you could use some warm food? Let's go back to our camp and eat." Daniel says holding out his hand. Tiffany claps her hands and hurries after Daniel, as Toby walks with the others. "Where are you from or where were you going?" John asks as they make their way out of the building.

"We were in our basement for the longest time at home in Wyoming before we were raided and had to make a run for it. We loaded up all our food, water, clothes and whatever our old truck could carry. Dad just took off, we drove north as far as our gas would take us and then we walked and walked until we came here." Toby takes in a deep breath, "we have been here for about two months, then our food ran out, so we broke open all the machines and after that we had no choice but to eat the rats." He shivered, "that's when mom and dad left us to find other shelter and food. But I hate to say it, but I think Tiff is right, they were killed by raiders or died of thirst or starvation." Toby sniffs and looks at the men.

John pats his shoulder, "well, that's quite a story.

We can be your new family now?" Tiffany nods then waves to them as they enter the camp. "Toby look, real food and warm tea, yum." She giggles drawing her knees up with her arms around them. Her green eyes dancing in the fire Daniel just made. Toby takes a carrot and munches away greedily then he licks his lips and looks for more.

"How old are you two?" Daniel asks, "I think we will be 13 at our next birthday, but I am not sure, I have lost track of time." Tiffany shrugs taking another carrot. "Well, lets get some rest we have a two day walk back to Silver Haven," John says. Tiffany and Toby huddle together as John puts his blanket over them, pulling up his jacket collar and leaning into the fire.

Morning comes and Dan is already up making tea and stoking the fire. John is sitting up on top of a rock gazing out over the horizon. Dan stares at Tiffany sleeping, "once she is cleaned up, she is really a pretty little girl." He smiles as she stirs and then wakes Toby. "Toby which way did you say your folks were going to go again?" He thinks for a minute then looks up at John.

"Well, we came south from the east. I think I heard dad say they should head west toward the setting sun." John jumps down from the rock. "Okay, then lets make our way back going west. We will take the long way back to camp."

"They left three weeks ago through the dock entrance." Toby says taking a cup of tea. "OK, that is facing west, so that's where we will start back. We will make a loop around then cut back north to the camp. It's about three days this way." John says packing up his things and getting ready to leave.

By nightfall they make camp as the sunsets. Tiff and Toby eat and fall asleep instantly. They don't have much strength. "I want you two, to take the kids back to Silver Haven. Brett and I will continue west for another day or two, and then we'll head back to camp. Just to see if we can find them." John says to a nodding Dan and Damien.

In the morning John and Brett are gone by the time the kids wake up. "They went to find your mom and dad." Daniel says to the twins. "We will head home now, OK?" They nod and get ready to leave.

By late afternoon John and Brett come across tracks and follow them to a cave in the side of a hill. They slowly make their way inside with flashlights on.

"Nothing inside, however, it looks like there had been someone or something sleeping here." John says, "See how flat and brushed away this area is, as if sweeping the rocks aside."

Brett nods, "this is promising let's keep moving, there is still another hour or two of light left." John nods and they head out once more continuing west. In another hour they come to another rock formation and decide to camp for the night.

"One more day west then lets turn back south and head home." Brett says pulling out some biscuits. As the sun rises, John and Brett are already on their way. But they don't have long to walk before they find a woman leaning up against a fallen dead tree. John walks up slowly, "she's dead," he says looking up at Brett.

"Her husband can't be to far off." They take the time to say a few words and John removes the woman's bracelet and ring, before they cover her with rocks. "I'll give these to Tiffany."

Brett nods, smiling sadly, "I think she will like that." They move on by early afternoon, and soon come across tracks that appear to be dragging. They approach cautiously and spot the man up ahead, laying face down in the dirt. He had been dragging his coat and empty canteen, "yes, he is dead too."

John and Brett drag him back to his wife and take off his ring and find a pocketknife for Toby. They bury him next to his wife. Then turn north and head back to their home, a two days journey. Daniel and Damien finally make it back to the entrance of Silver Haven with their two new family members. It is already dark as they give the password, "Mother Earth."

The boulder rolls open slowly as Matthew stands at the entrance wide-eyed and mouth agape at the two little rag dolls standing beside the brothers. "You better take them directly to Sarah."

Daniel nods taking Tiff's hand, "come on, and let's go see the doctor first thing." They both follow in silent exhaustion.

"Sarah, we have two new patients for you." Daniel says cheerfully. Sarah looks up, "Oh my goodness, where did you find these poor babies? Come on children, and let's have a look at you." She holds out her arms. They both run to her crying. Sarah mouths, "thank you," and nods. Dan winks and leaves her to care for the twins.

"Let's get you all cleaned up first, OK?" Then I will have a good look at you." She takes two large towels and leads them to the pool.

Tiffany takes one look at the pool and squeals with delight, pulling off her boots, she then dives head first into the water. She begins to toss out her clothes piece by piece, as she swims.

"Come on Toby, its wonderful." He smiles and slowly takes off his boots and clothes. "He is so thin," Sarah thinks, as he wades in. Tiffany splashes him and he jumps in after her laughing. They swim around for a while then Sarah hands them a bar or soap. "Wash up good, or I will do it for you, OK?" She smiles.

"Yes mum," they say in unison. Before long Tiffany emerges dripping wet. Sarah wraps her in a big warm towel. "We are going to have to cut your hair, sweetie, its just to tangled up."

Tiffany looks up at her and smiles, "whatever you think, Miss Sarah." She turns to look at Toby, and hands him a towel.

"Thank you, Miss Sarah." He dries his head and wraps it around his waist as he climbs out of the water. They follow Sarah back to her area and they lay down on a cot while Sarah takes her time examining them both carefully. She cuts their hair short and gives them some vitamins, milk and a biscuit.

"When you're done eating, lie down and go to

sleep." The twins nod and watch her leave. Sarah can hear them whispering as she walks off to find Martha. The kids finish eating and lie down, falling to sleep instantly.

"Martha, have you heard of our two new additions?" Sarah says as she walks up to Martha and puts her hand on her shoulder.

"Yes! I did. 13 year old twins." She says with a smile of the great news. "They should start school tomorrow, I think. Other than a little malnourished and a few cuts and bruises, I think they are fine. I have started them on some vitamins and they will be taking extra meals at noon for a while." Sarah smiles and says, "good night."

Martha makes two new places in the classroom for her new students and sets out books, paper and pencils for them. She is excited for her new pupils and she thinks the other children will be pleased to have new playmates.

The next morning at breakfast Tiffany and Toby are introduced to everyone, and their new classmates. Everyone is happy to meet the new additions and their new classmates take them to school. Everyone waits for Brett and John return, to hear the news about the new twin's parents. They fear the worse has happened.

The following evening Stan gets the password at the entrance and rolls the boulder aside to allow them inside. "Well?" Stan asks hopeful. John shakes his head. "We buried them together." They walked off toward the dining room. Sarah, Martha and Esther are having tea, when John and Brett walk in looking drained.

Martha says nothing, just jumps up and rushes out, then hurries back with hot tea and warm buttered bread. "We buried them out there together." John says sadly. "Martha when the time is right can you give them these things from their folks, I think they would want to have them."

She looks at the handful of jewelry and knife, and nods with a sad smile. "I know it will mean a lot to them and I will talk to them and try to help them understand." She leaves grasping the things in her hands.

Chapter 6

The newly adopted twins adjust quickly and put on weight and become healthy and happy. Everyone makes Tiff and Toby part of the family and they both respond well.

Martha is pleased with their grades and they love helping with the animals.

Days go by and everything has fallen into a comfortable routine for the twins and everyone seems to adjust well to the two new little people. Tiffany is just a joy to have around and Toby is starting to come out of his shy shell.

Martha takes the twins to a quiet place to talk to them about their Mom and Dad. She explains softly about what happened the best she could and handed Tiffany her Mothers jewelry and Toby his fathers ring and knife. They sit for some time together talking softly as Martha leaves them for a while to absorb the details. Tiffany seems to be all right with it, but Toby is having a hard time adjusting to the fact they will never see their parents again. He gives his sister a hug and they walk back to the animals together.

"Aaron," I whisper into his ear as I roll over and hold him. "Honey, it's been one month to the day that we married, happy anniversary!" I kiss his shoulder then his lips sweetly. "I think I am pregnant."

Aaron's eyes pop open. "You think, or you know?" He turns over and faces me. "Well, I am very regular and I am almost two weeks late." I say smiling and kissing his nose. "Aren't you happy? I think its great and I am so excited. But I will give it another full week, before I go, and see Sarah. Then we can announce it to everyone."

We lay in bed for a while longer holding each other, talking about names for the baby. "I need to get up and help mom and dad with the big harvest today. I will see you at breakfast. I love you."

"I love you too, Rach." Aaron says watching me dress and walk off toward the gardens.

Mom, Dad and Leah are already picking tomatoes when I arrive.

"Grab a basket and lets get started, we have to pick all the vegetables by the end of the week. So they can be canned, pickled, stewed and dried at the peak of ripeness." Mom says bending down.

"David and Jane are anxious to get started on the soups, stews and other preparations for all the food we are picking." Dad says wiping his brow with the back of his gloved hand.

By breakfast we finished the tomatoes and washed up to eat, then we are back to the gardens. Aaron sits and eats with us and then takes his turn at guard duty.

"Everyone Martha and I have an announcement," Joseph says proudly drawing her up to his side. "We plan on getting married next month." They both blush as everyone starts to cheer and clap.

"It's about time you two." I shout cheerfully. Joseph waves me off, blushing`.

"I had to ask him." Martha confesses as she laughs and everyone joins in.

"That's wonderful news," my folks say together as they hug each other. "One more to go," dad says chuckling, looking at Leah. She blushes and shakes her head, "no way."

Everyone who does not have other tasks helps with the harvest until dinner. Then we all walk into the dining room to eat dinner together. "We are going out again after the harvest is complete." John announces at dinner, glancing around the table.

"Can I go this time?" Stan asks. "Sure you can, Stan. Brett, Damien and I are heading east and I am not sure how long we will be out this time. Our map is getting pretty good but east still needs some work." John says standing and drinking down his tea before leaving with a plate for Matthew on watch.

The rest of the week is uneventful until mission four is ready to head out. They pack enough for a week and start for the entrance, when Sarah rushes up with the medical kit.

"Sorry, John I almost forgot it." Sarah says looking up into his strong face. He smiles, "I knew you wouldn't. She blushes and gives him a hug. He kisses her cheek. "See you in a week." John waves and the foursome heads out for another mapping adventure.

The foursome travel fast and hard due east all day. They finally come to a large rock formation suitable for camp. Damien builds a fire and Stan helps fix dinner.

"It looks like a storm brewing." John says checking his compass and gazing at the sky.

The wind picks up by dark and the four sit back and watch the light show. Within an hour the sky opens up and the rain starts pouring down. "It's a acid rain and we need to cover up the best we can. We are going to get soaked clear through. Make sure all the gear is well wrapped and pile the rocks on everything." John orders, opening up a tarp and throwing it over the four of them as they wait out the storm. It rains for hours and the lightning is relentless. They are cold, wet and hungry by the time its slows down.

By dawn the rain has subsided and the morning turns gray with a drizzle.

Everyone shakes it off, but things are to wet to build a fire. So they chew on jerky and pack up, continuing their trek east. It turns cold so they quicken their pace to stay warm. In the distance are rolling hills so they decide to make the foothills by nightfall.

"Hopefully, it won't rain anymore. I am still wet." Brett says.

"Well, at least your boots aren't soaked through." Stan says almost whining.

"We will build a fire when we camp and dry out,

Okay?" John says grinning.

"Hey Stan, wasn't it you who begged to come along?" Damien says kidding him. "Yeah, yeah, yeah." Stan says pouting.

They make it to the foothills by dark and look around for a place to set up camp.

"Hey look over there, up to the left, it looks like a cave." Brett says pointing it out.

"Okay, let's get up there and check it out, but be careful." John says taking the lead. They hike up the hill slowly, because it's getting real dark, even with the flashlights, the going is difficult.

Inside the cave opens up, they can hear water dripping further back. "I'll start a fire," Brett says as the other three wander slowly inside the cave.

"Hey, over here you guys." Stan yells, while his flashlight is poised on a skeleton. "I wonder how long this poor bugger has been here, it looks like his leg is broken." Stan stares at it.

John kneels down and looks through his pockets. "His name is, George Newsom, of Butte Montana." He pulls out a picture, "looks like his family." He gives the picture to Stan. "Yeah, poor guy, dying all alone like that."

"Not quite, over here." Damien shouts. They go down further to the left and focus on Damien's light beam. "Looks like three more bodies."

John moves in closer, "let me guess, wife, son and daughter." "I wonder how they all died." Stan asks kicking some rubble to one side.

Suddenly a large snake springs out at Stan striking

him in the thigh. "Shit", John it bit me." Stan yells falling backward to the ground as John moves quickly toward him and with one swift swipe of his knife takes off the head of the large rattler and tosses it against the rock face.

"Hold still Stan." John and Damien carry him back to the fire and break open the medical kit.

John rips open Stan's pants and draws his knife through the flames then makes two cuts quickly through the punctuate wounds. He then bends over and sucks out the poison, spitting into the fire.

Stan moans rolling back and forth. "Stay still, Stan. The poison moves faster if you move too much. Calm down, now." John says putting pressure on the wound. He then pours disinfectant on his leg.

"Ouch, that burns." Stan cries out. "Lay back and rest, Stan. Now we know how the rest of the family died." John says in a low voice.

An hour later and Stan starts to shiver and sweat, as John puts another blanket on him and a cold damp compress on his forehead. "We will stay here until tomorrow and see how he is doing. If he is still bad, Damien you stay with him while Brett and I continue on. When he is recovered enough to travel head back to camp and we will join you in a couple of days." John says as he takes Stan's pulse and gives him a drink of water.

They eat and drink then turn in for the night. It is going to be a long one. They take turns watching over Stan.

Morning comes and it is clear and things are drying out. Stan is still unconscious, so Brett and John eat and pack up, heading due east over the hills into another valley. Damien stays behind caring for Stan. He keeps busy by exploring the cave carefully, knowing full well it is probably full of snakes. But he thinks they make good eating and went hunting.

The following day and Brett and John slowly approach a small group of nomads in the valley among the dead forest. They see five men, three women and three children.

"John you keep an eye on them, while I circle around to the opposite end to see if there are others, that are on guard or look out." John nods as Brett moves invisibly around the perimeter of their camp. Slowly he moves closer and spies a young man in the rocks. Brett comes up behind the man, and puts his hand over his mouth and twisting his arm behind his back, making him drop his rifle.

"If you promise not to yell out, I will release you." The man nods. "What is your name, how many more of you are there and where are you headed?" Brett asks quickly.

"My name is Stewart, I am the only lookout and what you see down there is all that is left of us, out of 35 people. We have traveled up from the southeast, when we were ambushed. They were very heavily armed men, about 20 or more, I don't know for sure. Most of our men were killed. Nine of the women were kidnapped and two young boys were also taken." Stew takes a deep breath. "We are running out of food and one of the children is sick and one of the women is about to have a baby. We are in pretty bad shape, can you help us or do you plan on killing us?" Stew looks up into Brett's face and sees the kindest in his gray-blue eyes and Brett grins with a nod, "we will help."

"Go down to your group and explain carefully and slowly that there are some people surrounding you right now who are willing to take you to their camp and share with you, okay?" Brett says slowly watching Stew's reaction.

Steward nods with a grin and walks slowly down the hill to his group. Brett watches him talking to the eight adults. The men start looking around and the women hold the children close. Steward calms them down and reassures them.

It appears that he has convinced them its ok, and to put their weapons down, because that's what they are doing. Then they all put their hands in the air. Brett whistles loudly and starts down the hill, while John starts down the opposite side.

When everyone comes together there is silent for a long time, staring at each other. Finally one of the men speaks, "I am Todd, this is Jeff and you know Steward." He points to the people as he gives them their names. "This is James, Jimmy and Dave. The ladies are Faith, Joy and Ruth. Joy is about to bring a new member into our little family any day now. And the children are, Brian, Johnny and Amy. That's all of us"

John nods to everyone. Brett cannot take his eyes off Joy holding her large stomach. "I am John and this is Brett. Damien and Stan are one days walk west of here, so if you are all ready let's get started back, we can rest in the caves.

Everyone picks up their belongings and follows John's lead with Brett closing up the rear and Stew by his side. Joy starts to slow down by midday and Brett offers to carry her. She is a very petite woman of fair skin, blue eyes and long black hair. Brett finds her lovely. She accepts the help shyly and appreciates his kindness.

By nightfall they make it back across the valley to the opposite hill side. "Let's rest here for just a moment." John says as he walks around and shares his canteen of water with everyone.

Then slowly they climb over the hill to the cave entrance where John sees a small fire. "Good, there still here. Hello Damien, you up there?" John shouts.

"Yeah, John, come on up." Damien says waving a flaming stick.

"We've got company." John says as he enters the cave, followed by the 12 bedraggled strangers and Brett.

"WOW! Where did you find these vagabonds?" Stan says in a horse voice, sitting up slightly.

"How are you doing, Stan?" John asks kneeling down by him, checking his bandage. "I'll live, ready to travel by tomorrow I think." John nods, "good, lets all eat and get some hot tea, and we will leave first thing in the morning, after a good nights sleep."

"Be careful, that large sack is full of snakes, I

thought we could take them back for a meal?" Damien says with a smile. "It tastes just like chicken." He chuckles and stands guard over them all night. Everyone settles down and takes refreshments.

Then dawn comes in a beautiful hazy orange and pink sky.

With everyone awake and finishing their meager meal of a biscuit and a piece of jerky, they drink it down with a cup of tea and pack up to leave.

"Let's get a move on every buddy." Todd says to his group. "Come on Joy." She struggles to stand and Brett offers her his hand. "Thank you, you are so kind to me." She smiles with a nod taking his hand.

Stan leans on Damien's shoulder as they all leave the cave and head back to Silver Haven.

By nightfall they all make camp. "We will make Silver Haven by late tomorrow night, if we get an early start in the morning. It will be another very long walk." John says to everyone tossing food bags to Damien, one of the women offer to help cook.

Damien builds a nice fire, while Faith makes a stew from all the rest of the vegetables. They all sit down and eat, chatting about their experiences. Then Brett decides to cut the heads off all the snakes. The children watch, mesmerized by the snakes twisting and hissing as he does the beheading.

"They came at us from all sides. They were all big men with lots of fire- power, dressed in black. We didn't stand a chance." James says sadly. "We only had a dozen guns between us, and the women and children were frightened to death." James wipes his face.

"Joy's husband died in her arms and I watched my wife being carried off by two men." Todd says angrily, hitting his thigh hard.

"There was nothing we could do, short of being killed ourselves." Jimmy adds, "I lost one of my girls and my wife died the following day." He stares into the fire.

Things started quieting down as the children fell asleep quickly and the women huddled together close by the children. Everyone slept except John that night; he watched them through the night. He wonders if Silver Haven will manage with this extra addition to their already large family group.

In the early morning two of the women rise and wake the children slowly, dressing them for the days travel. They eat the rest of the food supplies and sip water from the last canteen. "This has to last us the whole day, Okay?" Brett says to everyone. They all nod understanding, and move out on their last long leg of their journey home.

The day is warm but not unbearable. The children don't make a sound and the women begin to slow. Some men start carrying the small children and the others keep up the even pace. They pass the canteen amongst themselves throughout the walk. Some drink others choose to wait, to make sure the children have enough.

By nightfall Brett is carrying Joy again. She is asleep in his arms, leaning her head against his chest. In the moonlight he gazes down into her beautiful face and falls in love.

Damien leaves the group and runs ahead of them.

He gets to the entrance and gives the password, "Mother Earth."

The giant boulder slowly starts to open, just as the first of the group come up the path. "Wait, just one minute." Matthew says. John comes walking in with Amy in his arms. "Is there a problem, Matt?"

"Uh…err… No John, come in."

All 16 of them march in single-file. "Most everyone has already gone to bed, John. But I think Sarah might still be up." Matt says looking at everyone with curiosity.

John smiles saying "follow me this way." He waves his hand toward the dining room.

Esther, David and Jane are still cleaning up, as they all walk in. They look up wide-eyed. "David go get Sarah, please."

"Will do John, on my way." David says and quickly leaves.

Esther and Jane break out plates and cups for the hungry strangers.

They all sit down quietly as they are served, left over soup, bread and fresh melon. "This is so delicious, thank you." Joy says softly wiping her mouth. "How do you do all this?"

Esther smiles, "we grow it all ourselves, Joy is it?" Joy nods with a smile, holding her swollen belly. Sarah walks in with a medical kit, taking a seat next to Joy. "Sarah smiles, "any day now, by the looks of it.""

"Yes, I think so. I have been having lower back pain."

"No doubt all the walking has sped things up somewhat too." Sarah says putting a hand on Joy's belly. "The baby's father, my husband is dead." Joy says soberly. "Don't worry about a thing, I want to take care of you and your babies needs." Brett says standing behind Sarah.

Everyone looks up at Brett. "I want to take the responsibility for them, if there is no objection?" Brett says putting a protective hand on Joy's shoulder.

Everyone shakes his or her heads, some smile brightly. Sarah starts to look them all over one-by-one as they sit and eat. "The children could use some fatting up. And of course, Joy needs some special care but over all I would say they are in pretty fair shape. They all have a few minor cuts and bruises. And they all need a bath a hair cut and some vitamins too." Sarah smiles standing.

"We will find you all some fresh clothes, and you can all follow me to the pool for a bath, when your ready." Sarah says helping Joy up.

Everyone takes turn in the bath as their clothes are taken away to be washed, mended or burned, depending on the condition.

They all are given bed linens, fresh clothes and take a place around the pool to sleep for the night.

In the morning they will find more permanent places to sleep. They all will be assigned jobs to do and all the children will go to school. They will all find an active role in the growing family of Silver Haven.

CHAPTER 7

The early morning peace is broken by the cries and groans of Joy. "My water just broke. Help, Please."

Sarah comes running, "Shhh, it's alright, lets take you back to my area." She helps Joy up and they walk slowly back to her work area. She wakes Faith and Ruth as they walk by, "I will need your help, get towels, boil water, and assist me in the delivery of this baby." Sarah says as the women rise quickly and follow her to her quarters where there is an extra bed for the sick and the equipment she needs for medical procedures. The area is large, it's like their hospital and for recovery of injuries. This way Sarah can be close by and watch them easier. Her sleeping area is adjoining.

"Well, I'm thankful the baby waited this long." Joy says as another contraction grips her small frame.

Brett comes running over to them by the time they reach the bed. He lifts her gently on to the bed, taking her hand as she lays back into a pillow panting loudly.

Sarah smiles and hands him a bowl of cool water

and a cloth. "Wipe her face and hold her hand, alright?" Sarah instructs.

"We are going to prop you up so delivery is easier, OK?" Joy nods and leans up against Brett's chest.

"Ahh! Ouch... Joy interrupts the instructions with a loud cry as another contraction rips through her.

"Easy, Joy girl... Breathe, sweetness, breathe." Brett coaches.

Sarah smiles and examines Joy. "Oh!, my goodness. I think we are almost ready, this baby is not waiting." Sarah says dropping a large towel over Joy's knee's and readies scissors and her other instruments just in case they are needed.

"OK, Joy on your next contraction, I want you to lean forward and bear down hard." Sarah instructs as she spreads Joys knees apart. "Your fully dilated Joy, now come on and push..."

"Grrrrrr..." Joy grunts. "Oh yes, I can see a head, again Joy, push hard, girl...

"Here comes the shoulders, now push with all your worth, come on last time, Joy, push..." Sarah continues to coax.

"Well, well. Here he comes. Welcome to Silver Haven, little one." Sarah says raising him up for Joy and Brett to see.

"He is beautiful, Joy. What are you going to name him?" Brett asks as he wipes her face and kisses her hand.

"You name him, Brett." He blushes, "really?" Joy nods with a big smile. He thinks for a minute and smiles, "Bobby, after my baby brother, who I will never see again."

Joy smiles up into his gentle gray eyes, "Benson, for my husband."

"Bobby Benson, what a good name." Leo says and everyone starts to clap. The baby starts to cry and Sarah clips the cord and cleans him and then attends to Joy.

"You did real good, Mommy." Sarah says, handing the still crying baby to Joy.

"Congratulations, Joy." Everyone says as they start to go back to their jobs and duties. She nods thanks.

She drops the shoulder of her dress and suckles her new son. Brett watches them together and tears stream down his cheek.

He leans forward and whispers something into Joy's ear and she nods, yes, with a big bright smile. Brett kisses the baby's forehead then Joy's. He stands and walks over to where Sarah is cleaning up.

"Miss Sarah, would you do the honor of marrying Joy and I right now?" Brett looks proud and very serious.

Sarah looks at Brett then turns to Joy, "are you sure this is what you want?"

Joy says, "Yes, I would be honored to take Brett as my husband and the father of my baby. I think Benson would have liked Brett and would have wanted me to be happy and taken care of." Joy looks down into her sons face and tears trickle down her cheek. Brett's sighs deeply and waits.

Sarah looks back at Brett who is now beaming ear

to ear. "Very well, go stand next to your bride." She says with a wave.

Brett takes Joy's hand and Sarah starts a quick marriage ceremony. They both say, "I Do," in unison and kiss a long sweet kiss and then he kisses his new son.

"I now pronounce you husband and wife." Joy slips a gold ring off her middle finger and places it on Brett's left ring finger. "It was Benson's and I think he would have wanted you to have it." Joy smiles and falls back into the pillow to rest.

Sarah takes the sleeping baby, wrapping him and setting him in her bed next to Joy so she can sleep.

"I have watch in an hour and I need to eat. So will you please tell Joy I will be back as soon as I can?" Sarah nods, "will do, and Brett that was a very special thing you just did."

Brett blushes, "believe it or not, I fell in love with her at first sight. I did what my heart told me to do." He waves good-bye with a smile. Sarah just smiles, knowingly.

The rest of the day is spent in individual thoughts and everyone took a moment to go by and see Joy and her son. She informed everyone who paid his or her respects, that Brett was also her new husband. There was even more to celebrate. A marriage and birth all in one day and new comers too boot.

As evening falls, the dinner bell is rung and everyone makes there way to the dining room. Brett is relieved and brings his new family a plate of food and cups of juice.

Brett, Joy and Bobby share a quiet dinner together. "Can you take us back to our bed?" Joy asks softly. "Finish your juice and I will ask Sarah when she comes back, it's really up to her, she is after all the doctor." Brett says kissing her cheek. "She really knows best." Joy nods and smiles sweetly.

Within an hour Sarah returns carrying Amy. Joy is resting while Brett is holds his son. What's wrong with Amy?" Joy asks sitting up in bed.

"She is running a fever, but I am sure it's just all the excitement, I am just going to keep an eye on her for a little while. Oh and by the way, if you are up to it, you can move back to Brett's bed." Sarah says with a smile.

Brett jumps up with Bobby still in his arms. "Great, thank you, Sarah, for everything. Joy here, take my hand, I scouted out a new place for us to live and moved all my things there, so let me show you our new home." He says excitedly.

Joy gets up slowly and arm-in-arm the new family walks to there new dwelling. Brett had it fixed up nicely and even made a small bed for the baby.

"Well, what do you think? Do you like it? I know it's not much, but you will make it better." He turns to look at her. "Joy what's the matter, why are you crying?" He hugs her gently.

"It's wonderful, Brett. You're so good to us." She sniffs. "Here, sit down." He takes the baby and puts him into his little bed. "Let's talk for a while, alright?" Brett smiles taking her hand and starts talking about everything. About all the work around camp and everyone's duties.

Sarah examines Amy and notices that there is a swelling on her ankle with two small puncture marks. She suspects a spider bite of some type and puts a cold compress on it and gives her some liquid medicine to bring down the fever and swelling.

Sarah goes to make an announcement to the group, "We need to take all our bedding outside and give it a good beating and then bring in some of the chickens to the area to clear out any spiders or other bugs that might be hiding in corners. Make sure to shake out your boots before putting them on too. We might have unwanted guests, like black widows, or perhaps the brown recluse. I can not be sure, but we need to do it now, before anyone else gets bitten."

Her orders are carried out to the letter and everything is given the once over and aired out, which was needed anyway, by the look and smells of things. They did in fact find some spider webs and egg sacks which they destroyed and the hunt resumed for others through the night. They begin to keep an eye out for them and are more careful with all their clothing. The chickens were happy to scout out new areas for fresh food too.

The following morning at breakfast, Todd speaks up. "We would like to be added to your guard roaster. I speak for all of us." Jeff, Stew, James, Jimmy and Dave all stand up.

"That's great," John says, "it will make our hours on

watch less, and maybe we can start regular patrols of our outside area." All the men nod in agreement.

Faith stands up next. "Well, on the behalf of all of us we just want to say, thank you so very much for taking us all in and making us feel so welcome. So we decided to share what little we have with you too." She opens a bundle and hands them to Esther and Leo.

"This is for everyone, they are precious seeds, of various fruits and vegetables to add to your already wonderful garden." Mom and Dad accept the gift graciously.

"Then this old mantel clock for our dining room." Faith adds. "And then, of course, all of our weapons and tools." Todd interrupts.

John smiles, "I speak for all of us when we say, welcome and we are glad to have you in our family at, Silver Haven."

Brett stands next, "I would like to be excused from patrols and watch for awhile, to be with my new bride and son."

Everyone nods and claps. "Of course, Brett, and Aaron too because of Rachel his new bride. But don't get too used to it." John says with a smile. Everyone starts to laugh.

"Anything else?" John asks.

"Yes," I stand up and clear my throat. "Aaron and I are going to have a baby in eight months." Aaron takes my hand and stands beside me.

Everyone cheers and claps. I look over at my mom and dad and they are beaming proudly ear to ear.

"Okay, any other news? This has been quite the day

for surprises and announcements." John says looking around the room.

"Okay…" Joseph stands up, "Well, next Sunday after church Martha and I are getting married and we want you all there." He says embracing Martha who is blushing.

Once again, cheers and clapping resume. Then after a long moment of silence, John smiles and says, "O.K. that's it. So now every buddy can get back to work."

There is lots of chatter and laughter as everyone starts to leave and gets back to their daily chores and duties.

The day goes by and everyone enjoys the day with family and doing their personal things together and their usual daily chores.

The following Sunday morning church service, Sarah reads from the bible and talks about family. After services everyone stands as Faith and Ruth sing, "Here comes the bride."

Joseph and Martha walk into the dining room together. We gave her Esther's wedding dress and shoes to wear. John had found two silver washers and polished them up.

Sarah performed a short ceremony; they exchanged the washer-rings and kisses. "That is another family started." Sarah says to everyone. Mom starts crying, "One more child to go."

"Shh… Dad puts an arm around her and Leah just smiles.

"Don't worry about that for a long while, Mom. I am not old enough for that yet, besides there is not a boy I am interested in or one interested in me." Leah reassures Mom, chuckling. Then the three of them walk out toward the gardens together.

Sundays are usually for cleaning, laundry, bathing, and families. But there are certain things that have to be done every day. The animals need tending and the garden also needs attention. Meals need to be prepared and there always has to be a guard posted. Plus the candles always need to be changed. But they usually let the children do that. Other than that Sundays are our free day, for reading, painting, playing games and relaxing.

The class is planning a puppet show and they are making everything. The stage sets and puppets, it's a long project and it keeps the kids busy and happy.

A month goes by and everyone is fitting in nicely. It is summer, July by the calendar and things are comfortable and the men are getting primed for another patrol as they are now calling them.

"Any man with a wife and family is exempt from patrols, but is expected to take his turn at entrance guard duty." John says to everyone gathered in the dining room.

"Are we ready to go?" Todd asks at the entrance to the men approaching. "I think so," John says swinging the medical kit in one hand and an assault rifle in the other. "Wait for James." Jimmy says standing next to Damien. All five men say good-bye to Daniel guarding the entrance.

"See you all in a few days." John says heading up the patrol. He slips his mask on and walks over the threshold.

Everyone says there good-byes at the entrance and watch them slip through, wishing them a safe return.

A week goes by and no sign of the patrol that went west again. Everyone tries not to worry by keeping focused on his or her work and duties.

Everyone has his or her own thoughts, idea's, and concerns about the tardy patrol. They hope that everything is all right, however, there are was still those men from the prison to worry about, and all pray there was not any trouble.

Keeping busy is the key for their mental health and there was enough for all to do. It's just a matter of time before they return.

Our Sunday prayers are given for their safe return…

Chapter 8

"Mother Earth," Comes the password. David rolls the boulder slowly to one side. John is looking battered and tired.
"Where is everyone?" David asks concerned.

"We were ambushed by those convicts, Todd and James were killed. Damien took one in the shoulder and Jimmy took one in the leg. I just broke my thumb. Can you help them in?"

David drops his rifle, "sure, you bet, of course." He rushes out cautiously, looking all around. He comes to a dead stop as he sees the devastation for the first time. There is nothing but dead trees and dried up earth with rocks and boulders. He comes out of his daze when he hears his name.

"Hey! David we're over here." Damien shouts. Jimmy is leaning against him as they slowly hobble up the hill. David picks Jimmy up and carries him the rest of the way. Sarah is waiting at the entrance as they come inside.

The boulder is closed quickly. "We killed at least

ten of them, but they surprised us. I did not think they would venture out this far west. They looked half starved and crazed." John says leaning against the rock face.

Sarah eyes Jimmy's leg, she can already smell the infection, and she frowns.

Faith rushes up to help. She carries a medical kit too. She starts to treat Damien's shoulder. "The bullet went right through, you will be alright."

The following day we have a ceremony in remembrance for Todd and James. It was a quiet and reflective time.

Sarah ponders the possibility of Jimmy losing his leg, because it does not look good.

Faith walks up to Sarah, "I have had some experience with surgeries and procedures of this nature. May I assist you, Sarah? I was a licensed nurse."

Sarah smiles broadly, "You are an angel and perhaps a life saver. Are you thinking what I am?" Sarah opens the bandage on Jimmy's calf. The stench is certain of the infection and it is spreading.

"Let's clean it out and see what some antibiotics will do for a day or so." Sarah looks at Jimmy's pallor. "Jimmy, do you know what we might have to do to your leg?" Faith asks softly.

"Cut if off? You mean to chop off my leg!" Jimmy says looking very frightened. Faith kneels down beside him and takes his hand. "We will do everything we can, but first we need to get the bullet out, OK?" Jimmy nods.

Sarah starts and IV and gives him a shot of morphine. Next she gives him a sedative push as Jimmy slowly falls asleep.

Faith drapes a small sheet over his swollen calf and Sarah begins to prop around the wound and retrieves the bullet. She drains it and puts her strongest disinfectant in it. Then she bandages it firmly.

"Let's give it a day or two and see how things go. Faith please, start the antibiotic drip and then monitor him until he recovers."

She nods, "Will do, Sarah. Faith gets busy, checking his temperature and blood pressure hourly.

"He will be out for a few hours so I am going to get something to eat and some rest. I will bring you a plate back with me." Sarah says while she washes up.

"Thanks Sarah, that's very thoughtful" Faith says sitting down next to Jimmy and pumps up the blood pressure cup on Jimmy's arm.

The twins are in the kitchen peeling carrots and potatoes when Sarah arrives. "Can I get a plate of food for Faith and myself?" We missed dinner because we were operating on Jimmy."

Rebecca nods, "of course, Sarah. Renee can you dish them up some stew, please." Sarah smiles warmly as Renee hands her a tray with two bowls of stew, bread and two cups of tea. "Thank you so much."

"You're welcome," they say in unison. When Sarah returns Faith is changing his dressing and Jimmy is coming around. They eat and watch over their patient until morning.

The camp echo's with the cries of a baby as everyone stirs in the early morning hours.

Tiffany and Toby are already down with the animals. "Oh my goodness, Toby, Come over here, look." Tiffany points to a dead chick.

"Hmm, let's take it to Miss Sarah and see if she can help." Tiffany carries the chick to Sarah in her little hands. "Sorry children the baby chick is dead and it has been for while. See the insects on it." Sarah says pointing to the maggots.

"Icky!" Tiffany says in discuss. "We better get back to the animals before we get in trouble with Jesse. He has us doing special things to help him take care of all the animals. We are his assistances," Toby says proudly." The twins wave good-bye and leave.

"Hi Joy!" Faith says as she walks in to the infirmary. "How is Jimmy doing?" Joy asks quietly carrying her son.

"Well we took the bullet out but the infection is very bad." Faith says looking concerned at Joy, "are you feeling alright?"

Joy frowns as she walks over putting the baby down on Sarah's bed. She glances at the table and notices the dead chick.

"I'm doing fine, thanks for asking. You know if you take some of these maggots from the chick and put them on the wounded part of Jimmy's leg the insects will eat away the infection and bad tissue." She says in a matter of fact tone.

Sarah and Faith both are looking at Joy. "How do you know that?" Sarah asks looking rather surprised.

"I'm not really too sure, I think I read it some place

along time ago." Joy says shrugging her shoulders. "But it was done under sterile conditions in labs and I think the maggots were bred special for it, but I'm not totally sure." She smiles, and waves good-bye, picking up the baby on the way out.

"Well we have nothing to lose, let's try it." Faith says taking a bowl over to the table and removes some of the maggots from the chick. They then tell Jimmy what they plan to do.

"If it means keeping my leg, I'll try anything." He says sleepily. Faith smiles, "Good," Sarah says removing his bandage. Faith cleans them off and places a few maggots on his wound, and then Sarah places gauze over them. "We will change them tomorrow and see how things are going."

"OK, thank you ladies, for all your time and effort." Jimmy says as he falls back into the pillow.

The following day, Sarah and Faith repeat the process, out with the old ones and in with some new ones. By the following afternoon they start seeing some improvement.

They are all very pleased with the results and Sarah writes everything in her medical journal, for future reference.

John's thumb is much better and Damien's shoulder is healing nicely. All in all Faith and Sarah are very pleased with their work and new experiment. Thanks to Joy's comments, Jimmy is going to keep his leg.

Everyone is very happy to see the new medical team

working so well together. They feel very comfortable with the fact they now have two very able doctors on board, and doing great things together.

The boys make themselves a weight room to exercise and keep fit. It also seems to be relieving some stress and tension. All the men take turns at the equipment, even Toby and Jesse.

The days turn into weeks and another month passes. It's late August and I am starting to show. "Aaron the baby is due in February, maybe for Valentines day." I smile at Aaron. He kisses my cheek.

"Rachel, I have a meeting with the men in a few minutes, I will be back as soon as I can." Aaron says waving good-bye. "OK, see you later." I say as I continued picking peas.

"The reason why I called you all together is to talk about our convict problem. Sooner or later they are going to find out where we are. I say we should attack them and take them out. Hit them hard and full force, before they hit us." John says clenching his fist.

"I say wait them out, winter is coming and I don't think they are going to last. They looked pretty bad last time we saw them. There are only about 30 of them left, if that. I say wait." Damien says flexing his healed shoulder.

"All right, all right!! Let's take a vote, all in favor of striking now?" The count is six. "All in favor of waiting them out?" The count is eight. "Well then, I guess we wait." John says sitting down.

"All right then. In the meantime I suggest we start a

program of training and major weight exercises to prepare. Damien says.

"That's a great idea!" Stew says. "Yeah, I'm with you." Daniel says.

"OK, let's start tomorrow." Matthew says excitedly.

"Male bonding," Ruth says as she walks by. They all laugh.

Weeks go by quickly. Jimmy recovers and all the men are taking their training very seriously. They are all there at different times throughout the day and evening, depending on their shift on guard duty, and their other chores.

"The boys are really looking buff." Leah says to me one day in the garden.

"Yeah, that's true. Aaron is looking and feeling wonderful. "Even Jesse and Toby are filling out." Renee says as she and Rebecca walk in to get some vegetables. We all begin to laugh and continue chatting as we continue picking vegetables and fruit.

The following month rolls around and everyone is doing well. It's September and everyone helps with the harvest and canning. It's a good time and everyone pitches in with the gathering.

"Our ewe is having trouble delivering this large lamb, so get Sarah." Lynn shouts at Jesse. Sarah and Faith rush into the stall area to see the distress of the ewe. They both work for hours to help the mother deliver the baby. But with all their efforts the lamb is born dead. The children are very upset and Martha tries to explain that sometimes thing happen and they start to calm down. Daniel and Jesse take the lamb outside and bury it.

Joseph and Martha are enjoying married life. Their classes are doing well. The kids are all doing great. Tiff and Toby are excellent students, eager to learn everything. The new children are becoming excited about all the school activities. The first puppet show was a sell out and a total success. They decide to do another one. It is so much fun for the kids and everyone seems to really like the change.

One afternoon, John opens the weapon locker and calls all the boys together. "We need to clean and put all our weapons in order. Let's take inventory and clean every piece." John is pleased with their work.

"They all feel real good working on their arsenal, its very satisfying work." John said to Sarah one night after dinner.

"Well, it also keeps them busy and they are less restless that way." Sarah says leaning against John's chest, enjoying their quiet time together. "You are a good man, John." Sarah whispers.

Everyone dresses up for a Halloween Party and we all have a great time and it is a fun night. We play pin the tail on the donkey, dancing and hunting for candy and fruit.

The group is now working together like a well-oiled machine. Everyone has their tasks assignments and the projects continue for the big plans on attacking the prison early spring.

By November plans are made for a big thanksgiving dinner. Everyone pitches in. David and Sam butcher five large chickens, plus fixing all the mouth-watering trimmings. We all have a wonderful time and give thanks for our plenty and family.

The smells filter through camp and Dave on watch is taken a huge filled plate and a cup of cider. No one is left out on this great day. The children stuff themselves and play games. The laughter is a wonderful sound and we all enjoy our special time together. It is getting cold outside and it slowly creeps inside. It's time to use our precious generators for heating the main area of the encampments. We all dress warmer now and focus on next month. The ladies break out more socks, wool underwear, hats, mittens, gloves and sweaters.

The following week plans begin for Christmas. Everyone discusses all the details. "Our calf will be ready to butcher by next week and the beef will last us through the winter." Sam says.

Jane drags out a huge old cardboard box filled with all sorts of things. She pulls the tree out and puts it in the corner of the dining room. Decorations go up everywhere. It really begins to feel like a holiday.

Day by day people stop by the tree and hang ornaments they have made. The ladies make some out of yarn and bits of colored paper. The guys make them out of their metal, colored glass and items from scrape pile. They had some from last year too.

Mom and Dad candied cherry tomatoes. Then strung them on the tree, it looked wonderful.

Dad, Sam and David slaughter the calf the next day. It is all sorted out, packed, dried and will last all winter. But it was still a sad day for everyone. Tiffany and Toby were especially upset. Sarah had to explain the reason we had to sacrifices the calf, so we could survive. "Remember, these animals are not our pets, they are here so we can live. Do you understand?" She looks at them carefully.

"Yes, Miss Sarah." They say in unison. "But it is still sad." Tiff says wiping her eyes. Sarah gives them both a big hug.

By Christmas the camp is looking very festive and I am getting as big as a house. "Rachel, come and sit down. I will carry that basket of fruit." Aaron says to me. "I can handle it, I am not going to break."

"Well, Sarah said to take it easy." Aaron smiles, with love and concern. "All right, I will, but between you, Sarah and Mom, I feel like an invalid." I say rather sharply.

"We just want what's best for you and our baby. Rachel, just two more months sugar, hang in there." Aaron says sweetly.

Christmas morning is upon us before we know it and we are singing Christmas carols and light candles on the tree and up and down all the tunnels. We all sit down to a huge feast, with even pumpkin pie and whipped cream.

"Yummy, everything is so delicious. I am stuffed." I say patting my already fat stomach.

Everyone walks to the entrance singing, "Silent Night," and taking two plates of food and a cup of cider, tea and a big piece of pie to Damien on watch.

He even starts to sing, when we start singing, "Joy to the World." We all have a wonderful day and evening. We drew names for gifts. I got Sarah and made her a holder for her glasses, because she is always losing them, but usually there on top of her head.

I got a little mobile that will be cute for the baby. Aaron got a set of hand weights and everyone enjoyed the holiday. There were lots of candleholders and wind chimes made and given too.

We spent an hour together reflecting on the people we lost and the people we gained over the year. We toasted them all, with bottles of our precious champagne.

We stayed up late that night and sat around talking about everything. We sang every song we knew and ate candy and looked at everyone's gifts. The children played games and we all went to bed feeling just a little more thankful and happy to be where we are.

"Merry Christmas, everyone," Someone shouts as we settle down to sleep that night.

"God bless us one and all, please watch over us in the coming New Year." I say a little prayer before I close my eyes and roll over and hold Aaron tightly.

During the night I roll over and smell smoke, but I'm not sure if it's just a candle that has gone out or left over smells from dinner.

I get up and pad down to the dining hall for a drink of water when I see a flame flickering in the corner by the Christmas tree.

As I go toward the corner I realize the tree is engulfed in fire. I begin to yell, "Fire, Fire, come fast!" I run into the kitchen and carry out a bucket of water and throw it on the flames, it just spread the fire more.

By this time some of the men rush in with blankets to smother the fire. It takes a while to get the fire under control and we lost one of the wooden benches to the fire too.

Everything was full of smoke and we needed to open the front to air it out for a while with fanning blankets to push the fumes outside. We were all working hard all night to clean and clear the mess and smoke.

By having the entrance open for so long we lost most of our heat to the winter's night.

We rushed to wrap the children in extra coats and blankets and closed the door as soon as we possibly could.

It was such an ordeal and we were cleaning walls and clothes for days after that.

But with all of us working together we saved our home and family.

One day Jesse corners John and asks for a time out with the patrols. "Give it another year, Jesse. It is very dangerous out there and you are still a little young and inexperienced."

"But I have been working so hard, John. I need the chance to prove to everyone, that I can pull my own weight and do my part around here too." John nods, "you do, Jesse, we all know that, you do more than you know. Please be a little more patient, Ok?" John looks at his disappointed face and gets a shrug and nod, all right.

Jesse walks off kicking the ground, toward the weight room to work out some more and to punch the bag to take out his frustration over being rejected.

CHAPTER 9

"Ten, nine, eight, seven, six, five, four, three, two, one. Happy New Year!! It's the year 2201."

Everyone shouts. We celebrate with champagne and noisemakers that Jerry and Stan made for everyone.

We bring in the New Year with shared dreams and stories. The night goes by quickly, with singing and dancing. Everyone has a wonderful time spent together as one big party. We have another big beef roast from the Christmas calf and some great side dishes.

The following day is real cold outside. The winds have been blowing for hours. It has made it very cold inside too. The snow is over six feet deep in places. John and Damien go out just to scout the perimeter. As they regularly do.

There back inside, within an hour, shaking and freezing. "Nothing out there now, that's for sure." John says rubbing his hands together. "It's best that we wait now until spring to go out again, nothing would survive out there for long." Damien says shaking snow from his dark hair. John nods agreement.

"Let's get a cup of hot tea." Damien nods, "sounds good." John pats Damien on the shoulder. "See you later, Brett."

"Later guys," Brett waves and watches them leave as he closes the rock door.

Another month goes by. "Aaron honey, you better go and get Sarah." I say rather loudly, pushing on his back hard.

"Oh my god!, its time." Aaron shouts, rolling out of bed. He pulls on a pair of pants, pulling on his boots and grabbing a shirt. He races out of our quarters.

"Agh!" I cry out just as Sarah and Faith come running in. "I think my water broke an hour ago." I say as another contraction grabs me. "I wanted everyone to sleep as long as they could before I started screaming to loudly." I chuckle. "I know it's only five, sorry."

Aaron kneels down by me taking my hand. "Faith we need my instruments, a bowl of boiling water, ice cold water and lots of towels." Sarah says. Faith nods and rushes off, waking Ruth as she goes.

"Let's have a look at you, Rachel. Lay back and breathe through the pain, don't push yet, Rachel." Sarah says as she feels my belly and looks at dilation. "Oh, we have a little time yet, sweet girl. You still have a little time to go. Try to relax when possible and breathe through the contractions. Don't push, Rachel. They are about 15 minutes apart. We still have an hour or so, Rachel." I nod and close my eyes.

Faith, Ruth, Mom and Dad come in quickly. "We have an hour or so to wait." Sarah says to everyone, pulling my Mom aside. "I think we might need to cut a little, the baby is very big." Sarah frowns. Mom nods understanding from Sarah's comments.

Mom comes over to me and sits down on the opposite side of the bed. "If you do not open enough for the baby, Sarah will be cutting you some, it's no big deal, but there is some bleeding that might occur, Rachel. Do you understand, sweetheart?" She says taking my hand just as another contraction grips me.

"Ruth can you fix us all a tray of food and hot tea, please." Sarah asks softly. Ruth nods and scurries off.

"Oh, my god it hurts." I grip Aaron and Mom's hands hard. "Hold on tight, Rach." Aaron says wiping my face with a cool cloth.

"Breathe through them, Rachel. You have a ways to go yet." Sarah says as Faith hands her the scalpel and sets up her tray of instruments and other sterile tools.

An hour passes quickly with contraction only minutes apart now. "OK, Rachel, I can not wait any more, for fear of putting to much stress on the baby. I am going to cut you just a little bit and it's almost time to push, sweetie." Sarah coaxes.

By this time everyone in the camp has been alerted to the birth and the coming new addition to the growing family.

"Now push, bear down, Rachel." Sarah says excitedly. Sarah takes the scalpel and makes another small cut. "Push dear, push." Mom says eagerly awaiting her first grandchild.

"I see the head," Faith giggles. "The baby is crowning, Rachel, just a few more pushes now, hard.

"The pressure is so great, I can't, and it hurts." I scream with one big push. "I feel like I am going to explode, Aaron."

"All right, there are the shoulders, OK, Rachel one more big push now, come on…"

I strain and bear down as hard as I can. "Okay then Rachel, you can relax for a moment. It's a perfect baby boy." Sarah says, tying off the cord and cleaning him up, lifting him up for all to see.

"He is beautiful, Rachel. Ten little fingers, and ten little toes." Aaron says with a great big smile, kissing my forehead.

"With one final contraction and it's all over, honey." Mom says with a big proud smile.

"He is a big healthy boy, Rachel." Dad says kissing Mom's head. Mom starts to cry and leans into dad.

The baby begins to holler loudly, as Faith cuts the cord and wraps him up.

Sarah does a few stitches, cleans me up and finishes up with her examine. "Everything looks good, Rachel. Rest and take it easy for a few days. If you have any questions ask me or Joy."

Sarah says as she covers me, and Faith hands me my son.

"What are you going to name your new son, Aaron?" Dad asks and we all wait to hear.

"My father's name was Andrew, so Andy for short. Andrew Leonard Altman." Aaron says with a big proud smile.

"That's a good strong name, son." My Dad says

proudly.

The baby starts to cry and I hold him close to me and Mom actually helps me with the first bit of nursing instructions. It feels a little strange at first but then I see how eager my son is and it makes me smile and I feel this warm surge through me. It's a warm glow running all along my body. I swell with pride and love.

Aaron just looks at us with tears in his eyes and the wonderment of it all.

We all spend some very special time as a family, chatting softly and watching our new son.

Everyone congratulates us and returns to their duties.

Aaron stays with us as I nurse Andy and then I get some much needed sleep. Aaron watches over us for I don't know how long.

I rest peacefully after that wonderful ordeal and glad for it to finally be over. I smile drifting off to a deep sleep.

Wondering what his future holds for him and us…

CHAPTER 10

February comes and goes and at the end of March, John and his entourage of eager warriors decide they will strike on April first.

Six men make up the attacking force, John, Damien, Daniel, Brett, Matthew and Stan. They prepare for their trek to the gray fortress.

The six of them gear up with provisions needed for their mission. Nothing is left out. Their list is complete, checked and double-checked. The plans are gone over with a fine toothcomb.

Then the day comes for their departure. Everyone is there to see them off. My Dad is on watch at the time and opens the entrance slowly for the first time after winter.

"Please take care of yourself and hurry home to us, Brett." Joy says softly, kissing his lips holding their son. "Shhh, I will, my sweetness, you take care of our little boy." Joy stands at the entrance until the large boulder is rolled back into the closed position.

It is a gray misty morning when they step outside.

Its cold but most of the snow is gone. The sky is gray, orange and in the far off distance they hear thunder.

They march north for the entire day and stop to make camp in the foothills of the ridge. Just on the other side and across the plains in the next hillside, the prison and their destination. They eat, rest and talk of their strategy tomorrow.

At first light they move out to the top of the ridge. John scopes out the battlefield below carefully. There is no movement outside the opposite hillside. The prison walls look deserted. It looks abandon." John says turning to face his team.

"I say lets storm the place, guns blazing and let god sort it out later." Brett says, "Lock and load."

"OK, let's do it," Damien says doing the same with his weapons. Everyone makes ready and John gives the signal.

"ATTACK!!" John yells as they all run down the hill toward the prison. They are shooting their rifles and handguns running full steam, until they reach the entrance to the fortress.

"You three right and we will go left at the junction inside the tunnel." John commands firmly.

Damien, Brett and Stan race in and disappear to the right quickly. John, Daniel and Matthew go left and move through the cells one by one.

Damien, Brett and Stan head for the galley. "The place smells foul and looks empty." Brett says, pushing the kitchen doors open.

"P. U., it stinks in here." Brett says holding his nose. "Oh my God, who died in here?" Damien says gagging.

Brett kicks some pots and pans as he walks over to a large walk-in freezer and opens it. He jumps back suddenly, when a bloody skeleton of a man falls forward onto the floor. "Damn," Brett says startled.

They walk through the dining area and are awed by the sight before them. Half eaten corpses, body parts and blood everywhere.

"The stench is too much for me." Stan says and runs out throwing up into a pan in the galley. Damien puts his arm over his mouth and breathes through his shirt and takes another quick look around. Brett is right next to him and they both back out slowly.

"Cannibalism, they ran out of food and started eating each other, Gross me out!" Damien says coughing and gagging.

"Shit, I hope we never get to that point, what a terrible thing to go through." Damien says shivering.

They all walked back through the galley and headed back down the corridor. "What a sad experience this was." Brett says shaking his head. "It was way to gross for me to handle." Stan says holstering his gun. Damien heads for the junction, and they are all silent in their own thoughts and disturbed at what they saw.

They hear the others coming down the opposite corridor. "This place is completely deserted." Matt says as they join up.

"We noticed," Brett, says, "we also noticed what was left of the prisoners. Apparently they had to resort to cannibalism. We found partially eaten bodies, it is pretty discussing in there, John."

"Good Lord, are you serious?" Daniel asks shocked

at the report. They just all nod their heads in disbelief.

"It must have been bad?" Matthew says sadly.

"Well, lets see what we can salvage, and get the hell out of here." John says moving out quickly. "Fan out and pick up anything you might think of value, or useful." John instructs, with a wave of his hand forward. They spend the rest of the day looking through all the cells, rooms and doorways, finding only rats and cockroaches.

By nightfall they all join up at the entrance. Everyone is carrying a sack full of items. "Let's get out of here on the double. We will camp at the foothills of the ridge."

All six of them double-time it through the plains. All loaded down they start to slow up, breathing hard; by the time they make it to the other side. "Man I am glad to be out of that place." Stan says bending over, holding his side and panting.

They make camp, eat and turn in for the night; it's a long trek back to Silver Haven with all their booty. Their sleep comes slowly, thinking of the horror in which they experienced. Trying to shake it off to get some rest for tomorrow will be here to early.

The next morning the sun comes up and the men wake to the smell of biscuits and hot tea. Matt woke early and decided to make breakfast so they could get a jump on the day. They eat in silence and pack up quickly. "If we don't stop to eat again we should make it back home late tonight." John says moving out, taking the lead.

"Mother Earth," John shouts at the entrance in the pitch- black night. The boulder rolls slowly to allow them inside. They all drag their bags of spoils inside and go directly to their quarters. "We will meet first thing after breakfast tomorrow." John says, "Good night all, and good work men, get some rest." They all wave goodnight and head for their beds.

In the morning after breakfast has been cleared. John calls a meeting. "It was the worse thing I have ever seen in my life." Brett says as they all recount their experiences. The women are all in shock and shake their heads in disbelief. Most of the men want to hear every last nasty detail.

"It just goes to show you what happens when order is lost and there is no discipline. I wonder how many other groups wind up in this same situation. Thank god, for our team work, organization and friendship to all work together as a unit, as a family." John sighs heavily and walks off to reflect.

Later that day John's group goes through all the items they bought back with them. A few guns, some ammo, knifes, kitchen tools, a few pair of boots and some clothes that were in pretty good shape. Other odds and ends, things to add to there metal pile.

"Well, in a way I was disappointed, we did not have a fight." Damien says with a smirk. "Yeah, I know what you mean." Brett says cleaning one of the guns they bought back.

"Hey John, when do we take out next mission?" Matt asks sharpening a knife.

John sits down and strokes his beard, "in a hurry are you? Well, we need to decide what to do next. We know we are safe here now, so do we venture outside and broaden our territory or play it safe?"

By this time they are all sitting around talking about their next step. They talk about everything, the do's and don'ts and the pros and cons.

"It would seem that now, that we know our enemy has been alimented we should plan to widen our patrols. Perhaps we can travel beyond our mapped area and continue to seek out other pockets of people." John says as he turns and looks at everyone, looking at him.

"It all sounds good, but what about our safety in numbers and the women and children. I for one as before want to continue to be content with what we have." David says walking in from the shadows.

"Well, we will take another vote tomorrow and ask for volunteers for the next mission, which will be extended. I am going to turn in, see you all in the morning." John says and waves goodnight.

Brett goes to check in on Joy and Bobby. Aaron comes home to Andy and me. Things settle down for the evening, yet you can hear muffled comments and whispers for a long time. The debate over the new phase of our existence continues.

I knew in my heart that Aaron wanted to be right in the middle of it too. So I said, yes, with some reservations.

The next morning for breakfast we all joined in the dining room, taking a seat and waiting for the first comments.

"All right," John starts by clearing his throat. "We all are aware of the end to the prison problem and our limited mapped area of about only five miles in all direction. Don't get me wrong, I think that's damn good, however, we need to come to some decisions on whether to expand further out of our safety perimeter, with extended patrols." John says looking around the room, waiting for a long moment before Aaron speaks up. "We need to grow, explore and seek out others to share knowledge and perhaps move topside, at least during the summer months. We can not stay down here forever." He says with his hands on his hips.

"I agree," Damien says. "Me too," Daniel chimes.

"Okay, all who what to expand our patrols, stand up and sign up on this list." John says standing and signing it first.

All the men sign up, except for David, of course, and my father and Sam.

"All right then, we will take out five men patrols for two week periods or unless we find someone or something." John says folding the paper, stuffing into his pocket.

Fourteen men sign up. Jesse again asks to go, but John said, "Maybe in another year you can, but you can start watch soon."

Jesse perks up and sits down between his dad Sam and mom Jane. She strokes his head in reassurance, "there will be plenty of time for you to go out and explore, give it some more time."

"All the guys can stick around for a meeting of teams and schedules." John says as the rest of the group leave for their chores and other duties for the day.

"OK men, today is settling up our teams and rotation to start our training program again. The patrol veterans will be team leaders, myself, Brett, Damien and Daniel. We will go out in groups of five, for two-week intervals, once a month, until winter, which sets in about November through March. We will take our original map and expand it in all directions by another five miles. We scout out for any survivors, animals or useable items. Reporting back all information, and marking all new territory on the land as well as on our map." John takes a deep breath and sits down. "Any questions, or thoughts?"

"So when is our first patrol?" Jeff asks excitedly.

"When we all agree, we are fit for the task. I suggest you start today. And remember you still have your guard rotation on top of everything else." John says standing, "dismissed."

Everyone disperses quickly most go directly to the exercise room. It fills up fast with lines at the equipment. John starts instructing them daily on hand-to-hand combat and survival skills. Sarah begins all day classes on first aide.

Everyone trains and studies hard. They all take this very seriously. They all want to be ready for the first patrol.

Everyone else goes about his or her own chores, duties and tasks of everyday routine.

Joy and Rachel bond because of the babies, they find a lot to do and talk about. It keeps them busy and they set up a small area for a day nursery, with toys, changing table and colorful blankets and other baby items. The two boys are growing big and strong and appear to be very happy babies. We are blessed.

Chapter 11

September first and the patrol readies for departure. John, Michael, Joseph, Jeff and Daniel. They gear up with weapons, ammo, bedroll, medical kit and they each carry their own water canteen and food for two weeks.

They layer their clothes and make sure their boots are fit for a long hike. That afternoon they head north. They walk abreast for the first few miles. John checks the map regularly, locating the original five-mile markers. When they get to that point they decide to rest and camp for the night. Daniel starts a fire and everyone begins to relax except for John. He scans the distance in all directions from a small rise, deciding which way to go tomorrow.

The next morning, they are packed up and walking single file due north as the sun rises. Every mile they add their marking on the map and land with a marker. They continue on until they reach a slope into a ravine. At the bottom there once was a creek. As they approach they hear muffled sounds coming from the bottom. John signals them to scatter into the rocks. Everyone holds their breath waiting, watching and listening. Their weapons poised as they make the slow decent into the ravine.

They spot a cave in the back of the hillside, and another shuffling sound coming from inside the mouth of the cave.

John signals them to approach with great caution. The sounds grow louder with each step forward. There is a damp, musty smell rising from the entrance to the cave.

Suddenly there is a flash of yellow/gold colored ovals, as the sun hits the cave opening. Then there are other shuffling and muffled sounds then a growling noise.

As John nears the entrance he crouches down and peers inside. His eyes adjust to the dark and then widen at the sight of a large borrowing type creature. It is a cross between a huge porcupine opossum animal with long quills on its rough skin and a long naked scaled tail with spikes on it. He watches for a long time as the other men surround the cave entrance.

"It looks like we have come across a mutant life form. From the sounds inside, I'd say there might be a lot, maybe a nest. They must burrow underground that would explain how they survived. But what they are is something else again." John says in low tones to the men, as he writes down the find in his log, noting the place on the map.

"It smells like there is water down there too." Jeff

says leaning into the cave entrance.

"Be careful, Jeff." Just as Joseph says that a large spiked tail comes whipping out of the corner of the cave catching and slashing Jeff's legs. He falls backward into the rocks hitting his head and the men all open fire on the cave. There are shrieks and screams as the bullets hit their marks. John gives the stop signal and Joseph rushes over to the injured Jeff, pulling him back to safety.

Joseph examines the damage, "the wounds nearly server his legs at the knee's, and he is loosing a lot of blood." Joseph quickly takes his belt and he tries everything he can think of to stop the bleeding by putting truncates right above both knees. Joseph administers morphine and wraps them tightly. He removes his jacket and covers Jeff, who is now shaking. Joseph then examines his head, it has a gash, but not to bad, he cleans and bandages it and just stares at Jeff for a moment.

"Let's move back to the opposite side of the ravine and re-group." John says as he helps Joseph carry Jeff.

The group is real shaken up. Daniel quickly starts a fire and they all stay alert and watch over Jeff.

They grab some sleep and eat in silence. They take turns on watch through the night.

"It's going to be a long night and things look pretty bleak for poor Jeff. I really doubt whether he will make it through the night let alone back to Silver Haven, even if we carry him, John." Joseph whispers. John nods, "I understand, and I think your right. We will stay put and see what happens." John pats Joseph on the shoulder, "you did all you could, and it's alright, it's no ones fault it was an accident."

The next morning they bury Jeff and John says a prayer. "Shall we check out the cave or return to Camp?" John asks.

"Lets check it out, but for gods sake be alert." Daniel says.

They all nod their heads in agreement, and soon they are slowly approaching the cave once more.

"Careful guys, be ready for anything." John says at the mouth of the cave. The musty smell filters up to their nostrils, a mixture of water, dirt and blood.

"Easy," John says as Michael takes the lead, walking in along the damp rock face, its dark and dank inside. They all turn on their flashlights at once. Something scurries off deep inside the cave.

"Michael gives the stop signal. "What do you want to do?" John whispers as he closes the gap between them.

"Let's go in." He gives the forward signal. "Watch out, I've got your six."

Michael continues further inside, he walks down an incline the surface of the wall feels damp and slimy. At the bottom is a small trickle of water, he cups his hands and tastes it, "Its good fresh, cold water."

Suddenly he hears something and slowly moves down closer. Turning his light to the right, he catches another tunnel, something moving inside. Slowly he proceeds toward the tunnel, he steps on something and it crunches. Then things start falling on his head and in his hair. He scans the light down and sees thousands of insects scurrying everywhere, including all over Michael.

"Ahhh, shit!" Michael yells running back out of the cave, covered in all kinds of bugs. He flails his arms about into the opening of the cave. Everyone runs out after him quickly.

John takes a blanket and starts hitting the insects off the dancing Michael.

"Oh God it awful, it's a nasty feeling." He says striping off his shirt and pants. They are all over him, as Daniel takes his clothes and starts to hit them on the rocks.

"Ack, that was so gross." Michael says still brushing his arms and legs. Everyone starts laughing.

"Those creatures must have been eating in there. That appears to be a food source for them." John says examining some of the insects. There is lots of protein in these bugs.

"Yeah, and I saw three more in there too, but the creatures took off as I approached, they truly don't seem to be dangerous. I think they might have been protecting their food supply and maybe their little ones." Michael says, pulling on his pants after another good shake. "Let's leave them alone." I think they are basically harmless, but I will make a note on the map and I think we can put a marker with a warning on it at the edge of the ravine.

"Well I say lets head back tomorrow, going east then back south." John says sitting down and chewing on some jerky.

123

The morning is warm and they begin their trek east by south east. After five miles east they turn due south and head home.

"Hey!, over there." Daniel shouts, pointing further east, "looks like a building, shall we?" Daniel asks with a grin.

"Sure, why not. That's what we are out here for, right, to explore?" John says swinging his rifle over his shoulder.

They head out toward the structure. By noon they are upon it.

"Looks like an old barn and farm." Daniel says starting the search of the area. "Sure enough, it's a farm alright." He says as he side steps a bale of hay and looks at an old tractor. He puts down his gear and starts to tinker with the engine.

"Hey over here," Michael kicks a large barrel drum. He un-screws the lid, "smells like gasoline."

John tosses down a block and tackle, tools and chains from the loft. "Dan, can you get that thing to work?" He says climbing down the ladder. "If you can we will take a few good bails of hay and the fuel with us."

"I think I can with a little time, maybe clean it up and prime it otherwise it looks like it's in good working order." Daniel says with a smile wiping his face smearing grease all over his face.

Everyone looks at him and laughs.

While Dan works on the tractor the rest search the surrounding area. They come across an old farmhouse that has collapsed and a well. "Here," tossing Michael a bucket. He ties a rope to it and drops it into the well. "It's pretty deep." They finally hear a splash. Michael starts pulling it up. He tastes a little. "Yuck, it's no good." Michael tosses the bucket back down. They wander the area scouting out useful things to take back to camp for a few hours.

Suddenly there is a loud pop, cough and smoke pours out of the barn. Then the tractor rumbles out of the doors. They all rush back applauding.

"Way to go, Grease monkey man." Michael shouts as they start piling everything they found on the back of the tractor.

"This is great we can drive back to camp." Michael yells over the roar of the large engine.

By nightfall they are back on track with only a couple of miles to go to reach Silver Haven. They decide to camp and wait for morning to make it the rest of the way.

They make camp and eat, sitting around the fire reflecting on their patrol. "One death, one discovery of a new life form and the door prize a honest to god working tractor plus a barrel of gas, not to mention all the other good finds. That is quite the accomplishments for one weeks work." Joseph says soberly.

The next morning turned cold, so they hurriedly loaded up the tractor and wheeled homeward. A full week had passed when Sam hears the sound of an engine outside the entrance. He would never open the entrance until he received the proper signal. Sam yells at, David and Leo passing by to come quickly. They wait patiently and Sam is nervous, when he finally hears the password.

The boulder is rolled open and everyone peers out at the large contraption. Sam smiles, "well, that's quite a find."

Michael jumps down, "and gasoline and hay too boot."

The patrol has lots of help unloading the tractor. Then they move the tractor to a more secluded spot out of prying eyes.

"Here Dan, Michael, help me cover the tractor with this camouflage tarp." The three of them unfold the large netting and drape it over the tractor. "There that looks pretty good, no one will see it unless they are right up on it." Joseph says standing back to inspect it. They finish up outside and they all walk inside and close up the entrance good and tight.

John goes off to find, Jeff's original group. "Jeff didn't make it, I'm sorry. We did what we could for him. We encountered a mutant creature and it struck out at Jeff before we all could react, but we kill quite a few of them. Plus we found a working tractor and brought it back with us, with enough fuel to last some time.

The men all nod acknowledgement; it could have been anyone of them. It's the chance they take when they go out on patrol and they all know that. They all talk together for a long time.

Joy holds Bobby and cries at the news; Ruth and Faith just sit down quietly holding each other.

At dinner that night, John informs everyone else of the patrol. There is a long quiet pause, and then John continues. "Our next planned patrol is October first, going west-south-west."

This time Aaron stands to lead the patrol. Matt, Damien, Brett and Stew stand up. "We're with you Aaron, they all say loudly. After that report and dinner finished, everyone but the patrol disperses.

"All right guys, lets get our plans and training up to par for our assignment in three weeks." Aaron says as John passes on the map to leader of patrol two.

The five of them get busy. The next three weeks fly by and before they know it, its time to leave. After all the good-byes they are ready to depart.

CHAPTER 12

The patrol begins to move out heading due west. They reach the five-mile marker as the sun starts to set. They decide to call it a day and get and early start for the new frontier in the morning.

By daybreak they are all up and ready to head out. Aaron checks the map and points in the direct to go. "We will continue west for another, five-miles then cut south and back around again." Every mile they mark it and make the notes on the map. This goes on for the entire morning. By the end of the tenth mile they all take a break.

Then suddenly out of know where, appears this large shadow from the sky. Everyone looks up to see a dusty brown glider and a single grey haired male operator. It soars around them and then disappears behind a distant bluff. "Come on lets see where he's headed." Brett yells, gathering up his belongings and running west. He makes it to the bottom of the bluff with everyone close behind.

There is nothing there but the rock face or so it

seems, "Who goes there friend or foe." Echo's this thunderous sounding voice from above.

"Friend!," Aaron shouts back, and then waits and waits. They all finally hear metal straining to open a door in the side of the rocky bluff. A single man appears.

"Greetings and Salutations!" Welcome to my humble abode. Please gentlemen, won't you come in."

He is an old man, long gray hair and beard. He has a tall straight back, curious blue eyes and a pleasant manner. He chuckles, "I have not had a visitor for, hmm, well, lets see… about three years, I guess." He chuckles again looking at the men with curiosity. "Oh, forgive me, how rude, my name is, Horace." He reaches out and shakes hands with all five of them.

"Sit down, would you like a drink? I distill it myself from potatoes." He says with a grin.

"Sure, Matt spouts as he sits down on a stack of readers digests. "Let me introduce my team", Matt says. "This is Aaron our fearless leader, Brett, Damien and Stew." He says pointing to each guy. They all nod with a grin at their names.

The old man nods to each one in order. "Well, this dwelling is warm dry, large and has its own water supply. Horace says motioning around the room with his hand. He hands each man a cup of cider.

"I have lived here alone now for almost three years, ever since my beloved wife died." Horace says sadly.

"We saw your flying machine and were curious, so we followed your direction." Aaron says glancing around.

"I scout out my surroundings everyday when the weather permits, hoping to see something or some-one." He smiles and takes a big swallow.

"It's nice to have company." He refills his glass. Stew takes the first sip. He starts to cough and gag.

"Whoa, easy, young man," Horace says patting his back. "It's a little strong for first timers." He chuckles.

Brett laughs and takes a sip. "Wow! I'll say, it's like moon-shine or corn liquor." He says taking another sip.

"Yap, that's actually what it is. I grow the potatoes right back there." He stands and motions for them to follow.

They all stand and walk back to see his garden, mainly potatoes, roots and mushrooms.

"In the spring I will grow other vegetables up here." He points up. There is a large over hang with steps leading up and a large glass covered opening for light. "To the right there is a funnel opening for the cook stove smoke.

All the comforts of home, except a family." He says sadly. "Well you're very welcome to come back with us to our camp." Aaron says, and everyone nods agreement.

"Well, thank you boys, that's a very nice offer. How about I think about it for a spell?"

The boys go back to drinking and sharing stories with Horace all night. Horace serves a nice hot home cooked meal. The evening is spent very pleasant and everyone sleeps on the floor in the warm hospitality of Horace.

Come morning and the weather has turned cold. The boys pack up and get ready to go. "We have a four day haul back to camp from here, if you change your mind here's our map coordinates." Aaron says shaking the old mans hand. All the boys give Horace a portion of their meat, as a gift, since he has not had any meat for over three years, and they all say good-bye.

The patrol heads out, as Horace stands at his entrance and waves good-bye, until they vanish.

They walk back to their original mapped marker. "It's a little further than we had planned, but we met a friend and mapped more area." Aaron says stuffing the map inside his shirt. They continue on their trek until nightfall.

It's been two weeks, two days and Rachel is very worried. She walks up to the entrance holding her son. Leo is on duty.

"Hi Dad," She says giving the baby to him, the baby squeals with delight at seeing his grandfather. Just then they hear the words.

"Mother Earth," Rachel nearly jumps out of her skin. Leo hands the baby back to her. She is so excited to have her husband home; she can hardly wait until the boulder is moved aside.

Leo opens the entrance and all five men stroll in smiling and no worse for wear. Rachel runs into Aaron's arms with a big hug and kiss. He takes his son and kisses his head. "I love you and missed you so much. We are both glad your home."

They walk into the dining room arm-in-arm,

where everyone is just finishing up dinner.

Joy smiles brightly and runs to greet Brett. He takes her into his strong arms and lifts her up spinning her around, kissing her lovely face. "Hello baby doll, where's my boy?" He looks around and spies him on a blanket. "Hey there, big boy," He picks him up and they walk off quietly together.

"I will see you later. I need to report to John." Aaron says handing Andy back to Rachel with a little pat on her fanny. He leaves followed by, Matt, Damien and Stew.

They inform John of every detail on their patrol and go over the map. "Well done Aaron. Now go spend time with your family, I know Rachel has been a nervous wreak." John smiles as Aaron leaves with a wave.

The following morning at breakfast, John informs everyone of the report he received from the patrol.

"His name is Horace and he lives alone in a bluff about 15 miles west, southwest from us. He has a flying machine and he makes very strong spirits." Aaron says with a chuckle. "We have invited him to come and visit or stay with us, but so far it appears he has declined, however the offer stands."

He looks around the room and everyone seems fine with that news. "Our next and last patrol before winter is November first. I will be leading this one, who goes?" He waits.

Jimmy jumps up pulling Dave. "I will too," Jerry says quietly. John looks around the room, "one more."

"OK, I will." Michael says leaning back in his chair with Lynn frowning, sitting next to him.

"All right then. We head out in two weeks, two days from now."

Everyone begins the plans for a long winter, they make sure the fuel lines are in good order, all the batteries are charged and the tunnel candles are refreshed daily by the kids. The women bring out boxes of sweaters, coats, scarves, gloves, socks and hats. They check them over very closely and repair any damage or clean any of need.

November first comes in with a cold raining day. They all dress for the cold weather. They are heading south by southeast. "See you all in about two weeks." John says waving good-bye giving Sarah a wink.

The patrol heads out into the chilly morning. By noon it has stopped raining and warmed up some. They locate the five-mile markers to the south.

By nightfall they make camp just inside the ten-mile south direction. They mark it and map it and settle down for the night.

Morning comes to the smell of a fire and they all start to stir. John goes over the next phase of their journey, turning east for another, five-miles. "The map is getting very good and lots of details, but it still needs to be expanded. I think I will propose a one-month excursion next spring. We need to grow and start living topside, at least in the spring and summer." John says stuffing the map into his shirt.

They ponder the new ideas and set off east. The

cold winds bring in a snow flurry, so they sit it out in some rocks.

The next day turns real cold so they quicken their pace east, noting every detail. Another large hill and then flat for as far as the eye can see. There is nothing east of the small mountain range, except brown dead earth and now snow.

John notes it all on the map then turns his attention back north and Silver Haven.

The following day they swing north again. The rest of the trek back is uneventful and rather disappointing. By the time they get back to the camp entrance it is snowing real hard.

When they have all entered Silver Haven and sealed the entrance firmly. They turn around are greeted by none other than the old birdman, Horace. "Hi boys, welcome back." He says with a toothless grin. He helps them with their gear. "Getting cold out there, so I thought I would take you up on your offer and stay someplace friendlier and warmer for the winter." I even brought my still," he laughs and does a little jig.

John smiles and shakes his hand as they all get settled. "It's getting pretty bad out there. I'm glad me made it back when we did." They all go their own directions and get some rest.

The following day they make their reports to everyone at breakfast. "We are in for the winter, but I think come spring we will extend our patrols even further."

Everyone listens to the reports and finishes up their meal and head out to do their assigned chores and they all settle in for a long winter. The winter routines take hold once again and before they know it, its thanksgiving again.

Thanksgiving is a big a fare once again, with four large stuffed chickens and so many different fruits and vegetables that everyone walks away patting their stomachs content, they even get to experience the Horace special. There are a few tipsy people trying to walk around, but it is all in fun.

The kids all go and play games and the adults talk about the idea of moving topside in the spring, it is a very exciting and dangerous thought, but one that needs to be discussed in great detail.

By Christmas spirits are high and everyone is preparing for another big holiday and feast. Joseph and Jerry surprise everyone with a metal Christmas tree. The decorations go up once again and people drop off items to hang on the tree and it is so lovely.

At dinner one night, Michael stands up with Lynn by his side. "Well we finally decided to get hitched on Christmas day, if everyone will join us." The couple blushes and hugs each other, as everyone claps and congratulates them.

Christmas Day and the snow outside is piled high. There is singing, drinking and a marriage. The Christmas dinner is a wonderful sight to behold, a dressed pig with all the holiday trimmings and spirits. The traditional gift exchange and singing.

They toast the new couple and dance the night away. The day and evening is spent in wonderful harmony with family and friends. It is another wonderful holiday.

"HAPPY NEW YEAR, EVERYONE!!"

Horace toasts and everyone shouts in the New Year 2202. Three years together for most of Silver Haven.

They have been through so much together. The rest of the day is spent talking about all their experiences. They each have their own memories and thoughts to share.

The kids put on another holiday puppet show and its enjoyed by everyone.

The rest of the winter falls into a quiet routine and family units. Horace finds his help best used in the garden with his potatoes and of course, keeping the still going. He has a big family to supply for now. He is a sweet addition to Silver Haven. Everyone has taken to him and consider him their grandfather.

The babies are growing fast and starting to walk. They are a joy to have at camp, especially during the duration of confinement of winter. They have become like brothers, since they spend so much time together.

Spring is in the air. Everyone is starting to get cabin fever.

By early spring at breakfast one morning, John stands up and makes an announcement. "We are going out April first for a one month long patrol far north maybe up to Canada and I only want single men to go with me this time." John calls out and waits.

Jimmy, Jerry, Dave, Stan, Matt, Damien and Daniel all step forward. "The rest of you need to stay to protect your families and keep Silver Haven going strong and productive." John says looking around at everyone.

"Well, we don't know what to expect but at least we know the convicts will not be bothering us. I think it is time also to take some of the planting and animals outside." Aaron says as Brett nods agreement.

"The tractor can really help with making a quick garden and all the children can tend the fields." Brett adds. "We need to plant grass for the animals to graze too."

John sighs and looks over at Sarah. "That should keep you all busy and your thoughts on something different. I will let Aaron, Brett and Joseph organize the outside project. Sam, David and Leo need to keep everything else inside running smoothly too. Remember you will also need extra guards outside also, so plan accordingly." John gets nods from everyone.

There is a new excitement in the air as they plan the next phase of their existents.

March 31, the patrol prepares for their long mission. They stock up on water, food, ammo and personal items.

The following morning they sit down to a huge breakfast. Everyone says their good-byes and wish them well.

They all walk the patrol to the entrance and wave

as they leave on a new adventure. They disappear north with John at the lead. Sarah goes back inside feeling very sad and worried. This is a long time away from camp with all the young men.

She wanders back to her quarters and says a silent prayer for John and the rest of his patrol.

They all spend the day in his or her thoughts about the out come of this long mission. Then they all turn their attentions to the new outside project that they are planning to take on, it is exciting and a little frightening for some.

They begin their plans for the topside garden. They gather up the necessary pipe, tubing for the irrigating. They put together tools and equipment to use outside for the new field they must help clear. "Hey, there are a couple of bags of grass seed by the hay" Jesse says with a smile.

The women find older clothes, boots and gloves for the dirty work and prepare water coolers and food baskets to be taken up daily. They talk about the way they are going to take the animals in and out. Plus the different food items they will plant, using the manure and water works.

All the arrangements have been gone over many times, but there are always things that need to be adjusted.

The guards need to be posted daily too.

CHAPTER 13

Their trek takes them far off into the distant uncharted territory where new adventures and dangers await.

John is a good and fair leader with plenty of skill and experience. All the men have traveled with him before and trust his judgment and advise. They follow his orders without question.

They passed the ten-mile marker in two days and head due north toward Canada to scope things out. The weather is clearing and warming up. The patrol is grateful for that. They hope and pray for no trouble but are prepared if it arises. The prospect of meeting new groups of people like themselves is exciting and promising as they continue their journey into the unknown wilderness of the new land scrape of mother earth.

Back at Silver Haven life returns to normal, minus eight men the camp seems empty and missing part of his family.

Aaron and Brett take charge of the outside arrangements. While Leo, David and Sam remain inside with the women to control the inside, it seems to work out well.

All the young people's thoughts move toward topside, so they swing the plan into action. They post Joseph and Michael as sentry guards at the edge and top of the mountainside and rotate the time on guard with Aaron and Brett. There will always be two armed guards outside during the time topside. They can see the entire outside perimeter from the two posts.

Joy and Rachel stay inside caring for the two infants and care of the daily things with Martha's help.

Esther, Janice and Jane take care of the meals and Ruth volunteer's to drive the tractor and she is very good at it. All ten children work the fields or tend the animals once Ruth gets it all plodded up. They let the animals wander the plodded field for two days so they have a layer of manure to spread out.

Sarah and Faith are there to help with any medial needs, or extra hands. They have to lay the pipe and tubing for the water system, it takes everyone's help.

Its hard, long hours of work but everyone seems to pitch in and enjoy their new surroundings and jobs. The air has cleared up enough by now, so they no longer have to wear the filter masks, everyone is thankful for that.

The main compound finally moves outside during the day the animals are let out, to wander around and stretch their legs.

It's the twin girls, Renee and Rebecca plus Lynn's

help to watch the large animals. They turn a hole in the ground, into a mud bath for the pigs and they love it. The cows munch hay and soon grass, they hope. The chickens scratch at the dry dirt, finding some insects.

Things start coming together nicely, and everyone seems pleased. At night everyone including all the animals go back inside. It's a chore sometimes rounding up all the chickens, but the children make a game of it, and soon the routine becomes old hat and the animals seem to like being outside.

They begin gathering large rocks and boulders to build a natural barrier to keep in the animals. It is made into a fun game by the children to see who can find the biggest rocks and how high and long they can make the fence.

A month goes by and no sight of the patrol. A few people begin to worry; some think the worse, others just pray.

"Maybe they found another group of nice people and decide to stay for awhile, I hope they didn't run into any trouble." Jane says to David one night at dinner.

Joy is pregnant again and Brett is very happy and proud. They are hoping for a girl this time. But as long as it's healthy that's the main thing.

Jesse is starting to work out a lot and taking an interest in Tiffany. Toby is working hard in the gardens and beginning to fill out. Leah has noticed him more and more.

The two younger boys, Johnny and Brian fight all

the time, but that is just a part of growing up in a close environment and boys will be boys. Ruth and Faith try to keep them busy building another enclosure around the field and it seems to be working. Toby and Jesse are helping too. It is looking very good and very functional. All their focus is on their new project, which is a good thing, due to the fact the patrol is still not back yet.

As June comes and goes everyone is very concerned and Sarah is going crazy about John. Rebecca and Renee pine for Daniel and Damien. Ruth and Faith pray every day for their safe return. And life goes on at Silver Haven.

The grass is starting to grow, thanks to the great seeds, manure and irrigation, Brett and Joseph put in, with the all the help of Jesse and Michael.

"Joseph, we are going to have a baby." Martha whispers into his ear, early one morning. "We are, are you sure?" Joseph rolls over looking into his wife's loving eyes. She nods her head.

"Oh, darling that is wonderful news, I am so happy and proud of you. Let's tell everyone at breakfast, Okay?" She nods again with a sweet smile. They kiss and get up, dressing and talking about names for their coming blessing.

Everyone still eats together and there is still a guard around the clock at the entrance, with eight less men, it makes it a little tough on sleep, but it is necessary for their continued safety they all agree to that. Jesse starts taking his turn at watch too, and is proving to be very responsible and mature about his duties.

Toby has asked for a turn also at the lookout post, but all agree he has to wait another year. But he can start guarding the entrance at night when everyone is back inside. He is very pleased with himself and feels very grown up and proud.

Dale is not interested in anything, he reads a lot and does puzzles but mainly he watches his sisters closely.

"There is so much more you can help with." Sarah says reassuringly. He agrees for now and goes about his chores.

"Everyone we are going to be parents in seven months." Joseph says happily. Martha just blushes as he takes her hand.

"That's great, Martha, we can be mothers of new-borns together." Joy says with a smile.

Everyone laughs and congratulates them.

"Hey Lynn, come on when is it your turn." Rachel says jokingly. "Well, tell that to Michael, I barely see him any more, he is always so busy." She says glancing at him, and he just shrugs.

"Sorry honey, I will try to be better." He says sheepishly.

Everyone laughs and finishes eating. They begin their daily routines outside.

By the end of July either they gave up on the patrol or become even more worried and upset. The ladies set up a prayer session in Sarah's quarters, it seems to help. But life still goes on. The animals are grazing on fresh grass, and they love it and seem healthier and happy and even putting on weight.

One day Horace decides to take his glider up for a spin and check out the area nearby. He returns a few hours later, with a frown and a shake of his gray head. "Nothing, not a single thing did I spy." The camps moral takes a nosedive after that.

Come August the fruits are starting to ripen and get big. Everyone's spirits seem to lift somewhat at the prospects of a great outdoor harvest next month. A nice and different change, from there usual routine indoor harvest.

The season's change and September arrives and everyone pitches in, to bring in the fruits of their labor. They cut the grass and there is so much. It seems more than there inside gardens ever produced. The seeds from the Faith and Ruth group produced lemon, orange and apple trees. That means fruit from them next year, if they survive outside this winter. The grape vines look promising too. Those are very special fruits to look forward to next year. They will wrap them in special plastic and pack them for the winter.

They all pitch in with the pickling, canning, drying and making as much as they can to keep over the winter. Potatoes galore thanks to Horace and his mushroom patch has gone crazy thanks to the animals donations.

Food aplenty and everyone starts eating three meals a day, especially the mother's to be and little ones.

Lynn squeals one night at dinner, "Well, it's confirmed, every buddy. I am pregnant!"

Michael falls off his chair, and everyone laughs. "Really?, Lynn, are you sure?" She laughs and nods, helping him up. He gives her a big hug, "I guess I did it, huh?" They laugh and hold each other. Everyone claps, laughs and give their congratulations.

Happy Halloween everyone!! The kids run around in homemade customes and make up. They have a great time with all the sweets they find. "Just think we can bob for apples next year." Ruth says with a sweet smile to the children. They all cheer and clap their hands happily as they run around.

The first snow comes around Thanksgiving. There thanks- giving dinner is a bountiful one but a quiet one this year, with lots of prayers and songs for the safe return of the boys. They had three large roosters with all the special Thanksgiving goodies.

Everything has been stored away for the winter and they make sure all the plants are well protected before they close up for the year.

At Christmas they slaughter one of their pigs and they have a huge feast and more prayers are said for their missing friends. We exchange gifts and play games. It is not quite the same with the emptiness everyone is feeling, especially Sarah and the twins.

"HAPPY NEW YEAR, 2203!!" Horace toasts. Everyone holds up a glass of his special holiday cheer. They all reflect for the safe return of their friends and a better year to come. There are a couple of the boys who drink too much, there is a little fight that breaks out, but everyone thinks they deserve it to let off a little steam and make little notice of it. They settle down soon enough.

The ladies break out all the winter clothes and so it goes, day after day, week after week and still no word. Some are forgetting, while they all carry on. They know it will not be until next spring now for the patrol to return so they try to make the best of it.

They all still have their jobs to do to keep things running smoothly and to carry on with their duties, regardless of their own personal thoughts and worries.

The children make daily rounds of the tunnels with a wagon of candles and matches. They make a game of it and pick up any trash and rocks in the tunnels.

Valentine's Day arrives with the cries of a new baby girl born to Brett and Joy. They name their baby daughter Angel. She is beautiful and healthy. They are all happy and healthy and doing great, with their growing family.

Mid March and another member is added to the family of Silver Haven with Martha giving birth to a healthy baby boy. They name him Scott, after Martha's grandfather. Joseph is so proud and makes a great father.

With renewed hope and prayers begin, as spring

approaches, with the new life brings and new hope for the future.

Everyone begins to prepare to go outside once again and start another season. They hope the trees and vines made it through the long harsh winter. They hope the wraps they put on them helped. Only time will tell. There will be a lot of work to do, with setting up again.

The routines and schedules for guard and lookout are put into place and the day comes to open the entrance.

Aaron and Brett take a walk around the area one afternoon just to check everything and make sure things are still all right and safe. It appears that things survived the winter with little damage. The rock fence needs a little repair and to be enlarged but the children jump right in with the games once more.

The fields are prepared for the tractor and the animals are readied for outdoors once again, they seem eager to be outside.

Chapter 14

April first one full year since the patrol left their home and loved ones. There is a special service held for them that Sunday.

Then they start the outside routines again and move all the animals topside. The tractor is fired up and Ruth hops up in the seat and begins the plowing. The kids start tossing rocks aside and make neat rows for the planting.

The water system is laid out again and they begin with the manure and watering of the field. It takes days to get it all set up for the seeding.

The chickens are out in force and there seems to be more insects this year, maybe from the large garden last year.

Everyone is tired, but feel that they are accomplishing a great deal towards, there future.

One day there is a group of people walking up the gorge toward Silver Haven. Michael signals danger, and everyone drops what they are doing and runs for the safety of the entrance, they grab what animals they can, closing the great boulder as soon as Michael slides inside. Most of the animals were all left outside, because there just wasn't time to bring them all in. Ruth had time to grab a lamb and Jesse scoop up a chicken. The sow was inside because she is due to deliver a littler any day. And there are still a few chickens, but all the rest are topside.

Everyone holds their breath and waits for what seems like a lifetime. They all listen at the entrance for noise outside. All the women and small children move further back into the cave.

There is a long dead silence and then, suddenly they hear a familiar mans voice call out, "Mother Earth."

Hope springs up in everyone's hearts as they slowly roll the boulder aside.

They all stand on either side of the entrance inside. They are just staring at the others outside for a long moment.

Sarah looks into the wise brown eyes and smiles, "John? Hello John, long time no see. Welcome home." She walks forward and gives him a long hug.

Rebecca and Renee push forward to finally lay their blue eyes on Damien and Daniel their heart pines for a year. They say hello and stay standing nearby them.

There are only those three they recognize the others are total strangers. John motions for them to go inside.

They all go into the dining room, after the boulder entrance is firmly closed and they are all offered hot tea.

"Where is my son Jerry, John?" David asks as Jane moves to stand with her husband to hear the news.

"He decided to stay behind at Dawson's Den, because he met a girl and she did not want to come. We lost Steward in the snow, but Matt, Jimmy and Dave also stayed." John says as he moves beside the new comers. "Let me introduce you to our neighbors to the north, about 300 miles that is."

He points to each man as he says their names and they step forward. "This is Marcus, Joel, Danny, Larry and Ted." They all smile nod and say hello in unison.

"They are all healthy, single men that were willing to come back with us to work and experience our way of life. They were all impressed with your outside animals and gardens. So are we, you all have done well in our absence." John says with a big smile.

Everyone says hello and introduce each other, then John takes them to find suitable sleeping accommodations. They each carry large backpacks and weapons.

"They are all tall with dark complexions and dark hair and brown eyes. They look a little a like, I wonder if they are all related?" Ruth says to Faith as she eyes one of them.

"That is a possibility, Ruth." They chuckle as they wander off together. Mumbling and whispers about the new blood.

The new comers take the boys beds that stayed behind and settle down. Almost everyone else goes back outside to resume his or her chores. Checking on the animals first then Aaron goes to stand guard topside.

Michael joins him on the opposite post.

"How is your place different from ours?" Toby asks curiously of the five men. Jesse stays to listen with curiosity too.

"Well, you have a lot more pretty ladies here." Marcus says with a chuckle and an eye toward Faith.

"We don't have anything close to your outdoor area, or not to mention all the animals. Unfortunately, we have a lot of dogs and cats." Ted says, pulling a little orange tiger striped and a black kitten from his jacket pockets. I brought them all the way for you.

"Ohhh!" Tiffany squeals as she reaches for them. "Here, there you're to take good care of. At our place they are a food source." Ted says watching their reaction.

"Oh, nooo!" Tiffany says loudly as Amy and Denise run outside with their new playmates.

"Well, they are actually a god send because ever since we rid our tunnels and caves of all the snakes the rats have taken over again. They have started eating our fruits and vegetables, but worse they are getting into the hay and grains for the stock." Ruth says as she watches the children go outside with the two new cats.

"Ok, so by Christmas if things go well you should have you're first littler. I brought a male and female, so not only do you have rat patrols in the near future but also if necessary a food source." Ted says with a smile and nod. "Just remember when they get older not to feed them too much then they will have to hunt for the rats for you and keep things in check."

"So what did you do mostly at your place?" Dale asks, as he watches his sister Donna following the girls outside.

"We were soldiers for camp and we are all cousins." Ted says. Ruth looked at Faith, "see I told you."

They giggle and it catches the attention of Marcus and he elbows his cousin Joel. The two wander off toward the two women.

Larry and Danny start working in the garden immediately. They seem to really enjoy the work. Leah and Donna watch them closely. As they whisper to one another as they work.

Ted jumps in the tractor and begins the plowing. They all work together for the rest of the day.

John and Sarah are quietly talking as he puts his things away. "I never gave up hope on your return, John. I always knew you would come back to me." She says as she watches him unpack.

"I realize that I love you very much, John." She sighs deeply.

He drops everything on the bed and turns to face her. Tears are streaming down his face. "I missed you more than I thought possible, I love you too." He drops to his knees in front of her. "I hope and pray you will marry me, Sarah?"

She starts to cry and kneeling down beside him. She takes him in her arms and holds him tightly, they kiss.

"You have know idea how long I have wanted to hear those words from you." She sniffs, "of course, yes, I will marry you." They kiss long and linger in each other's warm reunited embrace.

"Hey, you guys, it's about time you were getting back. We have been waiting for you two." Rebecca says with Renee nodding agreement and smiling ear to ear.

"Well, why do you think we came back, silly?" Daniel says walking over to Renee and kisses her nose.

"I thought of you every day I was gone, Rebecca. I love you, kid." Damien says holding out his arms. She runs into his arms and holds him tightly.

The four of them stand together holding each other for a long time, talking and kissing.

John and Sarah stroll by, "Okay you four, break it up."

The four walk over to them hand-in-hand. "We want to get married," the twins say in unison.

"Really? Well, so do we." Sarah says. "Tell you what, why don't we all get married together this Sunday?" She says, brightly, "I will ask Leo to perform the ceremony right after breakfast and Sunday services." She looks at the four young people then up at John with a big smile.

"Great idea!," The four say together. "I think that will be different and fun." John says as he and Sarah walk off together.

The day comes to a close up with everyone coming inside, including the animals.

The dinner bell sounds and everyone but Joseph is at the table. John stands and motions for the wedding party to rise. "Sunday after church, we all are getting married."

Everyone looks at them for a long silent moment,

absorbing the idea of all three couples getting hitched at once. Then in an instant, there are loud cheers and laughter heard throughout camp. It's so loud, even Joseph on guard hears it.

He smiles with a guess of what it is all about. "Leo, would you be so kind as to recite the ceremony?" He stands, "I would be delighted and honored." He says with a bow and a smile.

Janice stands, "Oh my goodness, my babies." David stands up next to her and smiles with a bow. "We thought you would never get around to it." Everyone begins to laugh.

Sunday arrives and the three couples stand before Leo. He says the words of marriage and everyone says, "I do," in unison.

"I now pronounce you husbands and wives. You may all kiss each other."

Everyone laughs and claps, the wedding party turns, holding up their hands. The party goes on all day. A few get drunk thanks to Horace special. The food is delicious and Janice bakes a large cake with fruit and cream frosting. Everyone dances and has a wonderful, reuniting and getting better-acquainted time.

All three men pick up their brides and carry them off to their private bedrooms and soon everything goes quiet.

Days later, a spring thundershower starts up and gets very loud with lots of lightning. The five new comers grab bags and go outside in the storm and are gone for a while. When the storm starts to subside, the five men come back inside soaking wet with smiles, carrying full bags and handfuls and pockets full of frogs.

"The heavy rains bring them out if you know where to look. They make great eating and a nice change to your diet." Ted says smiling.

"Here let me cook them up for everyone." He walks off toward the kitchen, with David and Janice in tow. Soon there is a wonderful smell of frog legs filters throughout the camp.

"Yum, they are delicious," Ruth and Faith say as they lick their fingers. Marcus and Joel join them and they laugh and chat together. There is Horace spirits serviced for a few adults who want some and the evening lingers.

Then Ted notices Larry and Danny walking over to sit by Leah and Donna.

"Hmm, there seems to be a pattern here." Ted says with a chuckle.

Everyone notices the new comers making themselves at home and finding mates quickly. They seem to fit in nicely and are accepted readily. Everyone seems to find jobs they like to do and begin to all work well together.

That night John and Sarah are in their sleeping quarters together. John slowly undresses his new bride. "You don't know how often I have undressed you in my mind." He slips her dress from her shoulders and she smiles up into his warm eyes.

"I too have dreamed of this time together. You have

made me very happy, my husband." She unbuttons his shirt kissing his chest. Her hands move down to his trousers, she unbuckles them and they fall to the floor. She kneels down slowly fondling his already erect maleness. She kisses the tip of him and swirls her tongue around the hard shaft. He moans softly, taking a handful of her ginger colored hair and gently pulling her up to meet his lips. They kiss in long, lingering, deep passionate exchanges. They caress each other a long time before he unfastens her bra and she lets it fall to the floor along with her panties.

She stands before him naked and they gaze at each other then into each other's eyes. Kissing once more, "You are so beautiful, Sarah. I love looking at you. I have waited all my life for someone like you. You're my dream come true," He mummers softly.

He lifts her up into his arms and gently lays her on their bed. He leans over her and begins to kiss every inch of her body.

He fines her erect nipple and begins to suck, lick and kiss her full soft breast. He slowly moves down her stomach caressing her as he inches along. Exploring the dark patch between her creamy white thighs he takes more time enjoying her womanly charms.

Sarah slowly relaxes under John's gentle touch. She lets her legs relax and John moves in to taste her sweet nectar. He inhales her scent and revels in her sounds.

She moves slightly under his tongues wandering through her folds and building desire. "Oh John, my dear, I have not felt like this in so many years."

He licks his lips and makes his way up to her lips

and kisses her deeply. "It has been just as long for me too, Sarah, I am sure." He muffles the words into her neck and buries his face into her hair, smelling her again. "You smell so good to me, but you always did." He looks into her eyes and they both smile.

They fondle, caress and kiss each other throughout the night, talking softly. Sarah finally reaches over and strokes him to hardness once more. "Hum, I suppose its time for the complete commitment." He gazes into her eyes and she nods.

Slowly he moves on top of her as she holds out her arms and draws him down to her embrace tightly. He enters her slowly and with ease from all the hours of sexual play. Beginning slowly he increases his tempo, "Oh Christ, Sarah, this won't take to long. You feel so incredible."

Within another two deep strokes he releases his pent up desire and passion, which he has held for her so long.

Groaning softly he lies down next to her and draws her to him. "I love you so very much my sweet, Sarah."

They finally drift off to sleep in a blissful, warm, loving feeling at last.

Around the opposite end of the pool in another small alcove the other two newly wed couples are sharing in each other's bodies as well. The sounds from their corner of the camp, is like animals in sexual play. They share one large area with blankets in between their beds. There is little to no privacy in camp with the now 41 inhabitants. So they all dig out a small nook where they can and do make the best of it. Most everyone is sensitive to this part of their lives and are given space when possible.

Their home becomes a very organized and professional camp. Things run very smoothly and everyone works well together as the days turn into weeks and weeks into months. Before long it is time to close up for another winter.

New relationships are formed and families are being built. The winter is long and they all make the best of being closed up. They have the usual holiday celebrations, at Halloween and the bobbing for apples was a big hit. Five large roosters with all the special Thanksgiving trimmings are set out. There is an announcement of another addition for next spring, and to the family continues to grow.

By Christmas the big metal tree is dragged out for yet another year, and festivities and decorations are out in force. It is a wonderful time with all the new family members. We all learn new things from one another and it's a very special time. A pig is roasted with all the special vegetables and fruits from the outside garden. Everything was delicious and everyone was full and happy together. Singing carols and dancing, with the usual gift exchange has now become a, Silver Haven tradition.

The children were all excited at Christmas because their two pet cats, Adam and Eve, just had four of the cuties kittens they had ever seen. So now the rat problem would soon be under control. By next spring they should have another littler and the rats will be on the decline. They have a contest to name the four new babies.

"HAPPY NEW YEAR! 2204, EVERYONE. PEACE ON EARTH AND GOOD WILL TOWARDS MEN AND WOMEN".

We toast with Horace special spirits of course and it is a very festive time by all. The dancing, singing and noise making was until dawn. It's good to be alive.

It's February, and there is another wedding and another reason to celebrate.

By spring John lets Jesse and three of the single boys go out on patrol to the west. They wind up in what is left of California, most of the western portion collapsed into the sea from the fault line, but they find a nice group of people along the new coast line in the caves and all decide to stay. They give their map and directions to three new people with letters to friends and family and the threesome make it back to Silver Haven, just in time for Thanksgiving. There is a big feast and welcomed celebration to the newcomers. They make there place in the fold and settle down with the Haven family.

They have another successful outdoor harvest and all is good for another year.

Christmas is another gala affair with all the usual festivities and great food and spirits.

Then comes 2205 and it's great to be alive!

They lose the families grandfather Horace the following spring and bury him under his favorite apple tree. Know one knows just how old he really was but every year they have a special apple cider festival in his honor. Plus they take his old trusty, dusty glider up for a spin.

From then on there are people coming and going to and from Silver Haven pretty regularly. New people are arriving, and others leaving wanting to start fresh elsewhere. Even a few go out for adventurer, in the new frontier. A couple of the men, decide to head out on their own as far south as they can go and see what they can find, in Mexico maybe.

The large government complex, NORAD, in the Cheyenne Mountains of Colorado, deploys troops to all corner of the United States, looking for survivors and making contact to establish lines of communication. They also start a count of people, and a new census.

They begin a mail service with some trucks that were still operational. There are lots of volunteers for the postal service. No pay just a place to call home and all the food and water you want. It is a very good thing for the young people, who want to be out in the new frontier. Most decide to ride some horses instead of the loud, smelly trucks. It is a big responsibility but there are many who want the challenge and are eager to be traveling the new country. There are still a few planes that are also used for mail but mainly emergencies and government work. Plus they can get around faster this way. It helps with the communication and keeping tabs on all the rest of the new United States of the Americas. The Canadians decided to make it all one big nation.

There is news from Mexico too, some want to join the Americas too.

New maps are created with details of the new cities and heads of towns, leaders, or council members of each group.

And so new family groups begin, new couples pair off, and new life is born. Even through the trials and tribulations of the planet being ruined, there are some that still survive and will begin anew and hopefully in a better world. They all try to work hard to make things better than before and all work together for a new free future for all.

It seems that only the smart and strong made it through the ordeal and perhaps now it will be a new start and they all will learn from the mistakes of the people that were lost.

It is a second, chance for our Mother Earth. We have risen from the ash, as people we learn from all the evil, wicked, corrupt ways of the past. It will take a very long time for the earth to forgive its children's misgivings and destructive nature. Yet, through it all, life goes on and the world continues turning.

Good luck and May God watch over all of us.

A new beginning

I WANT TO THANK YOU ALL for your continued support, and I hope you have enjoyed reading all my stories.

The Together Trilogy:
Forever Together
Forever Together Continues
Infinity Forever

Slave of Regulus
and
Silver Haven

Now I will take some time off to gather my thoughts and memories and begin working on my life story: "*Rachel*"

For copies of my books, please write to:

Rachel Baldwin
Forsbackagatan 24
SE 123 43 Farsta, Stockholm

Also check out my three poems on line at:

www.poetry.com
Under author, Rachel Ann Baldwin
My e-mail: rachel.baldwin@aurenav.com